The Collected Folklore and Poetry of Hen-Toh

The Collected Folklore and Poetry of Hen-Toh

Hen-Toh

MINT EDITIONS

The Collected Folklore and Poetry of Hen-Toh features work
first published between 1919–1928.

This edition published by Mint Editions 2023.

ISBN 9798888970034 | E-ISBN 9798888970188

Published by Mint Editions®

 MINT
EDITIONS
minteditionbooks.com

Publishing Director: Katie Connolly
Design: Ponderosa Pine Design
Production and Project Management: Micaela Clark
Typesetting: Westchester Publishing Services

Contents

Sketch of B.N.O. Walker

Written By Himself[1]

I was born in Old Wyandotte, now Kansas City, Kas., Wyandotte County. Am the youngest of a family of eight children. My father, Isaiah Waler was an eighth degree blood Wyandot Indian, belonging to the Ohio band of Wyandots, of the Little Turtle Clan. My mother, Mary Walker, was a quarter-blood Wyandot belonging to the band which long resided in Canada, along the Detroit, near old Fort Malden, of the Big Turtle Clan. She with her parents removed with her parents westward with the Ohio Wyandots in 1843.

I am of about three-sixteenths Wyandot Indian blood, a member of the Oklahoma band, of the Big Turtle Clan, in what was formerly Quapaw Indian Agency, now Ottawa County, Oklahoma. I say about three-sixteenths degree, for this reason: to give which it becomes necessary to go into traditional tribal family history. My paternal great-great-grandfather, James Rankin, and my maternal great-great-grandfather, Adam Brown, were white men (the latter a captive taken when a child in Virginia, and adopted and reared by a Wyandot woman) who both married Wyandot women, members of the band living along the Detroit. The women that they married were both of the Big Turtle Clan, known within the tribe as French women; since they were of French blood, descendants of a French Officer of the first fleet of French vessels which came up the St. Lawrence River, who took as his wife the daughter of the Chief of the village.

Two daughters were born of this union, and my two great grandmothers were descendants of these two daughters. My paternal great-grandfather, William Walker, was also a white captive from Virginia, who was adopted in the tribe and who married Catherine Rankin, a Wyandot girl, daughter of the aforesaid, James Rankin. Article Eight of the Treaty at the Foot of the Rapids of the Miami of Lake Erie, negotiated in September 1817, grants to "Catherine Walker," a Wyandot woman, and to John R. Walker, her son, who was wounded

---

1. The most of this article was written by Mr. Walker when he expected to have it placed in one of his books. It was never finished and was found in his desk after he passed away, June 27th, 1927.

in the service of the United States, at the battle of Mongaugon, in one thousand eight hundred and twelve, a section of six hundred and forty acres of land each, to begin at the northwestern corner of the tract hereby granted to John Vanmeter, etc.," said John R. Walker and a brother, W. W. Walker also signed this treaty as sworn interpreters. The treaty of Brownstown, Michigan, in November 1808, is signed by Adam Brown, my great-grandfather, as one of the principals of the delegation of Wyandot chiefs, and by my great-grand-father, William Walker, as one of the sworn interpreters. Great-grandfather Brown was also one of the signers of the Treaty of Fort Industry, July 1805, and of the Treaty of Greenville, August 1795. I mention these incidents to show that my people have been among, and influential with the Wyandots, for nearly two hundred years. When the War of 1812 occurred, Great-grandfather Walker and one of his sons fought on the American side, while Great-grandfather Brown in Canada, was with the British, to whom he always remained a loyal subject. I have in my possession, the faded scarlet gold embroidered flap from the pocket of his military uniform; also a pair of silver cups given him by Col'. Grant of the British Army, as a token of friendship and esteem. Until his death he was held as an authority on Indian affairs with the British, as also was Great-grandfather Walker and his sons so held by United States Officials, as to Indian Affairs in the Ohio Northwest.

When a child I removed with my parents from Kansas to Old Indian Territory, where I have ever since resided, except for the time that I spent in the Indian School Service, at other Indian Agencies. I was so employed in the Government Service, as teacher first, afterwards as clerk, from 1890 until 1917, in Old Indian Territory, Kansas, Western and Southwestern Oklahoma, California, and Arizona. I first attended school at a Friends Mission School established about the year 1872, near Wyandotte, Oklahoma. It was afterwards taken over by the Government and is now known as the Seneca Indian School. I afterwards attended the public school at Seneca, Mo., for a short time, then took up individual study for four years under an old College Professor who tried to establish an Academy in this locality. I then taught school for ten years, always doing a lot of individual study. Have always been a student and a reader. Was reared on a farm, and have always been a country boy and a lover of the woods and out-of-doors, doubtless an inherited trait. I greatly enjoy meeting people, but do not like to mingle in a crowd. My home is on the old place where my parents settled when they came to Old Indian

Territory in 1874, a portion of which was allotted and patented to me as a Wyandot Indian. My place is out in Oklahoma, about two miles southwest of Seneca, Mo., which place is our nearest town and post office.

I have lived among Indians all of my life, and have always been interested in everything pertaining to them. Have always enjoyed talking with the older people of the various tribes I have been among, and have thus made myself familiar with their "olden times," legends, myths, ancient customs, rules, manners, etc. And as I have told you that my ancestors have been among the Indians for several centuries, I guess that it is not either strange or remarkable that I should have been interested in these things. I recall my mother's telling me one time that when I was but a few weeks old, Tauromee, the last full-blood Wyandot chief, who was then leaving Kansas to come down to this country, came to our house to see me. He said to her in Wyandot: "Well, he don't look much like it, but he's a Wyandot, and he'll always stay with his people." The old fellow seems to have had the gift of prophecy, truly.

Concluded by Czarina C. Conlan

At the time of Mr. Walker's death he was Chief Clerk of the Quapaw Agency at Miami, and made his headquarters there. Yet he maintained his home at the old homestead six miles from Senaca, Mo., in Ottawa County, Okla. He was laid to rest in the old family burying ground near the home attended by hundreds of friends. He left two old brothers, Isaac and Thomas Walker, who made their home with him. A sister also survives him, Mrs. Mathew Murdock, of Senaca, Mo. Mr. Walker was fifty-seven years old and had never married. He had been in the Indian service over twenty-five years. A more loyal and true friend of the Indians never lived. Their interest were ever on his heart. He was never happier than when doing them some kindness or helping them over some of the problems that confronted them. As a natural consequence there was no man in that part of the state who was more loved by the Indians and the people in general. As a demonstration of the esteem in which he was held, while he was in a hospital during his last illness many of the Indians went to see him and were solicitous that everything possible should be done to save his life. They wanted his physician to have a specialist in consultation. One was sent for. When the case was diagnosed, he said everything was being done that could be, and he was ready to return to St. Louis. One of the friends suggested that if he could stay longer he might find something could be done. He was told if he remained another day it would be very expensive, in fact he would have to charge a $1,000 fee. Immediately the man took out his check book and wrote the specialist a check for that amount. All who knew Mr. Walker were aware that he had spent the most of his income for years in a beneficent way. He was in many ways an unusual man. Very versatile and talented. He could play the piano well and had a pleasing voice. He possessed literary ability, and had written an interesting book on "Tales of the Bark Lodges." A book of poems under the name of Hen-Toh. The history and legends of the Indians especially of his tribe had always been of great interest to him. Being a great student of history he had surrounded himself with a splendid library. In his old home were many valuable old relics of his family which he loved to keep as they had been placed there by his mother and father. In his library hung a large picture of William Walker, Chief of the Wyandott Nation, the first Governor of Kansas Territory, who was his great-uncle.

One of the priceless relics in the State Historical Society was placed there by him in 1924. It is a string of wampum from parts of the belts or tribal records of the Huron Wyandot tribes of Indians, the first people whom the early French discoverers met when they sailed up the St. Lawrence River. When the wampum was sent a note accompanied it. In closing he said, "May the wampum never again be removed, but forever remain in Oklahoma, the home of the Redman."

> *"Oh that whole wide world could now*
> *Accept the Redman's ancient symbol*
> *Offering its incense to the Universe;*
> *Bringing Goodwill to earth again*
> *With Peace, white Peace."*

> —Hen-Toh

TALES OF THE BARK LODGES

Foreword

More than a quarter of a century ago, among the scattered bands of the Eastern American Indians, were many of the older members of the tribe, whom we among ourselves called, "old time Indians." I refer to those tribes whose ancestors had associated with and known the white man and his ways ever since the earliest Colonial settlements were made.

Amalgamation with the civilized races had lessened the degree of Indian blood and they had become a civilized people. They were educated more or less, and were possessed of an innate refinement of thought and manner. They were reserved, closely observant, earnest and shrewd, and almost always serious. With all that they had gained from civilization, they retained and cherished closely, many of their old manners and customs, adapting these to the ever-changing times. They had a marked character and individuality of their own; and among them were those who, to a discriminating mind, were well worth knowing.

Many of these, however much they had acquired of the ways of others, failed in their use of ordinary English, to the most humorous degree. The greater number of them yet used their own tribal language, and they found it difficult to think something out in this, and then transpose and express it in English. Yet, in spite of the many perplexities, when in the mood to do so, within the family, or circle of intimates, the English language was often spoken to the exclusion of their own. And with all their natural earnestness and seriousness, they would drive straight ahead, paying no attention whatever to the strange and ludicrous quirks and turns they gave to English as they tried to speak it.

They lived much in the past of their race, and they delighted to talk and tell of "the olden times." Lore and legend were very dear to them; and during the long nights of winter, the traditions, tales and myths, handed down from one generation to another for centuries, were often related by these older ones.

I have always loved the old people and their olden tales, and in the broken dialect peculiar alone to the "old time Indian," I have attempted to give some of the old stories originally derived from the Lake Region Tribes. Since these have survived for unknown ages, and have been told and re-told to so many generations; and, since I and many of the friends I have known, have found a certain enjoyment in hearing them related,

I have tried to again re-tell some of them for the pleasure of anyone who may find in them anything to please. Perchance, even I, may thereby win another friend.

I have tried also to show somewhat of the individuality and viewpoint of these old people of the tribe; and it is to the dear memory of those who have long since passed beyond, and to the few that yet remain, that these stories and tales as now given, are dedicated.

Doubtless, there will be some readers, who will at once say that the rights and privileges of "Uncle Remus" have been set at naught. I say: not so; and I believe that my life-long intimate knowledge of Indian life and character entitles me at least to my opinion. Others may have theirs.

I can well recall the time of my boyhood, when I saw the first of the "Uncle Remus Stories." I was delighted with them because I found so much in them with which I had been familiar from my earliest childhood. I hastened to call the attention of the older members of our family to them. And, more particularly did I hasten to read some of them to a dear Old Aunt, a Wyandot woman of the old type, who lived with us.

Like myself, she was pleased with them, but at once said as many of the episodes were recognized:

"They're Indian stories; not whiteman; not negro."

I heartily agreed with her, and while we both enjoyed them, we were just a bit indignant because, so to speak, our title had been preempted.

Later, when the discussion was taken up by older and far wiser heads than mine, and when Professor Powell of the Smithsonian Institute stated that the stories exhibited more of Indian origin than of negro, I was satisfied as to my claim, and have never since had reason to doubt the fact of their Indian origin.

That the origin of many of the episodes is purely Iroquoian, is to my mind too clear to admit of doubt or dispute. The Cherokee is an Iroquoian tribe, as is also the Wyandot. The Cherokees removed south at an early day in the history of this country and became slaveholders. Can it be doubted that much of their lore, and many of their old tales and traditions were absorbed by the negroes? The Wyandots remained until years later, with their kindred tribes in the north, where these same stories, legends, tales, and traditions had been preserved, with perhaps slight variations among the several tribes, for centuries. Yes, even centuries before such thing was dreamed of, as the coming of either the white man or the black man.

Each of the many stories originally had some special significance which has long since been lost almost entirely. Their preservation was of tribal importance; and it was the duty of some of the older members of the tribe, to relate them to the younger ones. This had been an honored custom among them for untold ages.

Storytelling furnished a vast source of amusement and entertainment, as well as instruction, to the dwellers in the long bark lodges near the Lake shores, during the winter nights. Stories were never related except at this season of the year; for it was the belief that the many spirits of nature thought to be awake and alert during the other seasons, would be perhaps offended at hearing so much said about them. So, in the long, cold, and sometimes dreary winter season, when all nature seemed to be soundly sleeping, time was often whiled away, and even hunger and want forgotten while listening to a story well told.

Hen-Toh, Wyandot.
Ottawa County, Oklahoma.

I

OLD FOX GOES FISHING

What you sed, Bra-ty? Yooht! You all a time sed tell em Ol' Ouendot story. What for? He's 'bout all gone now, Ouendots. You jus' lit'l bit, you fatha', you motha' jus' lit'l bit mo' Ouendot. Look, you hair jus' lik' a sunshine if you ketch 'im an tie in bunch. Ouendot, his hair black like a night, an fine, jus' lik you sistah yonda. Eyes black too. He an you motha' an me, all looks lik' Ouendot." So spoke a pleasant, kindly looking old Wyandot woman to a little boy who was sitting with her before a cheery open fire, where a row of streaked, juicy red apples were slowly roasting on the broad hearth.

The boy replying to his Old Aunt, said:

"Yes, I know, but Neh-ah, I'm a Wyandot even if my hair is like what you say, and you know I just love to hear you tell me all of the old stories that the little Wyandot children, yes, and the older ones too, listened to so many, many years ago. That was before they ever knew there was such a thing as a white man, I guess. I like to hear all about the olden times you often tell me about, and how the Wyandots lived and did things then. Anyway, you know that as long as I can claim a little bit of Wyandot blood, I am an Indian, a Wyandot, and not a white man."

More than just a bit pleased, the Old Aunt said to him: "Well, I s'pose it's jus' that way, an it be that way too, all a time, with anybody what's Ouendot. Just say kin a proud, 'I'm Ouendot.' Anyway, I tole you all a ol' story what I think of, cause you all a time tell a me story 'bout nowa days, an read to me, book an paypa too, 'bout eva'thing what's goin' on in worl' an all a diffunt place. All a Injun long 'go use tell em ol' story, so young folk can le'rn all 'bout ol' times. Sometime when hunta's don' got back yet with meat, an mebbe so don't got much to eat in lodge, then jus' tell em' story long time, and jus' kin' a fo'got he's hungry. He's do that kin in a winta' time. But you don eva' much hungry; anyway look, we have good roas' apple, tzhu-u-wat, prit' soon. Well, anyhow, I tole you 'bout Ol' Fox an Ol' Coon, at's his couzzen. They jus' all a time try to play trick on each otha them fellas. Jus like long time go, young fellas what go all 'roun' diffunt village, an jus' play trick on ol' witch womans, an eva'body they could, an jus' make em big laff all 'roun' cause they foolish 'em, heap all a time.

"It's col' frosty mornin' long time go; winta' time. Ol' Fox he's lazy to get up, jus' sleep long time fo' he get up an go 'roun' to see what's goin' on. By-um-by, he's jus' walkin long riva' bank, jus' singin' like to he-self, jus' like he's feelin' kin-a-good. He's jus' come 'roun' by lit'l hill an he see Coon comin' up road. He's carry somethin' on back, jus' puffin' lik' its heavy. Ol' Fox he's wonda' what's got Ol' Coon. By-um-by he's come long clos, Ol' Coon, an Fox he see em long string, lots crawfish, what's carryin' Ol' Coon.

"Good mornin' Couzzen,' he sed it Ol' Coon, 'How you mek it? What fo' you sing jus' like happy, this time mornin'? Mebbe so it's gif you bad lucks, cause you sing so early. Mebbe so you bettah what you say, cut it out.'

"Ol' Fox he jus' grin an sed: Good mornin' Couzzen Coon, I jus' makin' up new song fo' nex' Council Fire; I don' tho't 'bout no bad lucks what you say; but what's you got, all lots a crawfish? Whe-e-e 'at's fine, how you ketch em? You jus' all time lucky hunta, ketch eva'thin'g easy; what makes all a time you do that way?'

"He sed it Ol' Coon: 'Oh, yes, me all time kill 'em ten. 'At's caus' you don't see me come singin on road befo' I eat 'em my breakfus; an this kin', I jus' pick em up down riva'. 'At's easy. Seems to me you can do bettah as I can, 'caus' you tail it's long an lots a-bushy.'

"Ol' Fox he think he's make a fun 'bout his tail, Coon, an sed it: Oh, it's good nuff my tail, but you don' sed how you ketch em crawfish; I like to try ketch 'em.'

"Oh, you lik' ketch 'em', Ol' Coon, he say, 'It's easy, but you haf to waitin' long time, jus' waitin',' but you don't haf to watchin' nothin', jus' waitin'.'

"Fox he say, 'Well, you tell a me, an I do what you sed. I lik' to try today, right now.'

"Ol' Coon he point back which way he come an he say: 'Right down on riva', 'roun' that bank, it's good place on ice, it's lots lit'l hole in ice, all ova'. You look, fin' good one, big nuff jus' put it in, you tail, jus' way down in wata'; he ain't cold much, wata'. You jus' sit there, tail in wata', waitin' long time. By-um-by, crawfish he come long l-o-t-s ov 'em, he get all tangle up on you tail. You jus' waitin' long time; afta' while it's feel heavy, but you jus' waitin' some mo an by-um-by when you waitin' l-o-n-g time, you jus' jump quick, jus' high lik' you can. You' tail it's be pull out hole, an it's all scattah ova' ice crawfish, lots ov 'em. You mus' pick 'em up hurry, fo' he's crawl back to that holes. It's sure bes' kin' fishin' I do long time. Sure ketch 'em plenty crawfish, mebbe.'

"Ol' Fox he's jus' lis'n to Coon talk 'bout it, an he say: 'Well, I try 'im what you sed, Couzzen, cause I lik to ketch 'em mo' what you ketch 'em, crawfish; I think I go try now.'

"Coon he sed: 'Well, you go try. I'm jus' 'bout froze it now, stan here tole you 'bout it, fishin'; nobody don' tole me, I jus' mek' 'em that kin' fishin'.' Then he's go on' jus' lik' he's hurry, that Ol' Coon. He's go lit'l way, an jus' laff to he-self, much, cause he's jus' fool'in 'im, that Ol' Fox; he don ketch em crawfish that way, lik what he sed it.

"Fox, he's jus' b'lieve 'im all of it; jus' cause he's got more big tail than Ol' Coon, he's jus' think he ketch 'em heap crawfish. He's go down on ice by riva', jus' hurry, cause he's want fin' hole, so he can do it, that waitin'. He's by-um-by fin' it good one, hole, but it's col' wind blow strong, jus' freezin', but he don care nothin' cause he's want try that waitin'. He's put in hole his tail, an he's set down on ice. That ice c-o-l', an jus' make sheever, jus' lik' eva'thin' He's jus' think it's be good eatin that crawfish, an jus' keep on sheever. He's don' care fo' that kin, sheever, he's jus' want em heaps crawfish.

"By-um-by, it's kin pull lit'l bit, his tail; it's freezin' that wata', but he don't know, he's jus' think it's much crawfish tangle on his tail. He's think, 'I jus' waitin' some mo' cause it's what mek 'em come lots crawfish. I sure beat 'im, Ol' Coon, ketch 'em crawfish, then I tell 'im, I bes' one fishin'. So that ol' feller, he's jus' waitin', an waitin' til by-um-by, it's his tail all freeze in ice; it's tight one, freeze, you bet'cha.

"He's waitin' lit'l mo, an sed to he-self:

'It's must-a-be many crawfish now, I think time to jump now.' So he's try to jump high, but it's freeze tight, his tail, an jus' pull h-a-r-d. He's jus' almos' holler, cause it's make hurt; but he's jus' think it's so lots ov crawfish, he don' care fo' lit'l bit hurt. He's jus' jump h-a-r-d 'notha' time, an it's almos' pull it off his tail; then he jus' think, 'He's foolish me, that Ol' Coon. He tell lie, he don ketch em this way, that crawfish; he's jus' lie all a time. He's do me bad one, this trick; but I'll pay back, I ketch 'im. He's fin' out.'

"Well, anyway, it's freeze up his tail, all tight plenty; what's goin' do get 'em loose, don know, cause it's hurt much eva' time he's try pull 'em. Jus' pull 'em h-a-r-d, it's 'bout break it, his tail. He's feel jus' b-a-d, now.

"By-um-by, he's lookin' 'roun', and see somethin' lik' black nose, right ova' tha' in hole, clos' to bank; then it's come up lit'l mo' an it's sharp eye, too, an Ol' Fox he's sed: 'O Uncle Beaver, I sure got it bad fix, mebbe so you help me.' Ol' Fox he's go 'head tell 'im, Beaver, what's that he's tell im do, Ol' Coon. He's tell im all 'bout it Ol' Fox. Beaver, he's jus' lis'n, an look like he's try hard not laff, an by-um-by he's go back in watah. He's swim ova' unda' ice, an he's work long time, jus' like eva'thin, and he's get 'em loose Ol' Fox, his tail; then he's come up top gen an tell 'em Ol' Fox: 'Now I guess you pull 'em out ice, you tail, my fren', an nex' time he's tell you how do somethin', Ol' Coon, mebbe so you don lis'n good.'

"Ol' Fox he's lis'n what'say, Ol' Beaver an think it; but he's want do something'g too, so he's sed it: 'Uncle, you come, I like fix it somethin' so I member it what you do.' Beaver, he jus' come ova' by Ol' Fox, an Fox he's jus' take hands an gatha up lots lit'l sof' white snow, an he's jus' rub it e-a-s-y all 'roun' it's his nose, Ol' Beaver. It's jus' change color lit'l bit that hairs 'roun' his nose, Ol' Beaver, an meks look nice, lit'l bit. It's jus' stay that way eva' since.

"That's how he say, Old People, long go it's that way."

II

A Dance and a Dinner

A nother evening when the Boy and Neh-ah were sitting before the same cheery fire, while outside the northwest wind swirled and whistled through the bare branches of the walnut trees, Neh-ah, knowing well that a story would soon be asked for, said:

"Bra-ty, I don' tole you 'bout how he's went to Big Council, Ol' Coon, is it? That ol' scamp, he's jus' know he betta' keep out his way, Ol' Fox, lit'l while, anyhow, caus he's jus' hope Ol' Coon, mebbe so, his couzzen he'll forgot it 'bout that craw-fishin', when he's prit' near los' it his tail.

"Co'se not, he don't fo'get it, Ol' Fox, an he don' tole nobody 'bout that kin fishin' neitha'; an' he's jus' hope Uncle Beaver wouldn' sed 'bout it to nobody too. But that Ol' Beaver, he's good ol' fella, and jus' heap like 'im eva'body; anyhow, he's jus' got tell 'im his fren' that Ol' Otter.

"That Ol' Otter, he's jus' jolly fella, an all a time jus' laff good 'bout all a kin a things; an that Beaver, he's jus' all a time likes to hear 'im laff big, so, jus' tell 'im eva' time, anything, that Otter.

"Anyhow—

"It's jus' few days afta' Ol' Coon tole it, his couzzen how to ketch 'em crawfish, he sed to he-self, Ol' Coon: 'Mebbe so I get out a way lit'l time, cause Fox he might try it somethin' to get even.' Anyhow it's jus' 'bout that time, it's come 'Rah-shu,' it's what you call 'em moccasin, he's go all 'roun' diffunt village, an tell 'em somethin', eva'body. He sed this one, it's goin' be Big Council way down 'notha place.

"Ol' Coon he's always like to go, cause he's good singa', an he's talk good sometimes, too. Anyhow he sed: 'I go, bet'cha Ol' Fox he's don' be there.' Then he's jus' laff, an he sed: 'I tell em all those fellas how's Ol' Fox he's ketch 'em crawfish.'

"So's he's get ready an' he's go. He's fin' lots of 'em that place when he's got there. Somebody he sed: 'Where is it Ol' Fox an Turtle, it's always come them fellas, wonda' where is it an why don come.' But afta' while Ol' Coon tell em 'bout how ketch 'em crawfish, Ol' Fox, he don say that no mo', jus' laff good.

"They all stay that place three-fouh days, talkin' 'bout lots thing, then Coon, he sed: 'Well, time I go, an he's pick up his lit'l drum an start back. He's jus' travel 'long all day, sometime he's sing lit'l bit, sometimes he's talk to he-self. He neva' see nobody, til he's jus' 'bout home, when sun, he's 'bout go ova' hill; then he's meet Turtle, jus' comin long slow, he's goin' home too.

"'Kway, my fren'!' He's sed it, Ol' Coon, 'What fo' you don bin there, Big Council? We look fo' you, all time, we want you make good talk.'

"Ol' Turtle, he sed: 'I goin' bin there, but jus' when I start, Ol' Fox, his woman he come my lodge, an he sed somethin' wrong Ol' Fox, he's bad cross, don' like nothin'. He want me come see 'im, Ol' Fox. So I tell 'im I go see Ol' Fox, mebbe so he's sick, I doctah him. So, I go see him, but I can't know what's mattah with 'im. He's jus' cross like dickens all time, an it's heap sore, his tail.'

"Ol' Coon he's jus' lis'n an laff lit'l bit, then he sed: 'Ol' Fox, he be a right in few day. I go, now, I gotta fin' suppa' some kin'.' So he's go on. By-um-by he's come out of bush, right by lake, oh it's nice one, that lake, jus' blue wata'h and jus' clos to sho it's swim 'roun' lots of goose; he's fat one, too. Ol' Coon, he's jus' look at those lots of goose, then he say: 'Yo-ho, my fren's, you come, I tell it you somethin'; where I jus' come, it's eva'body jus' sing an dance. It's new dance. You fellas jus' come out on nice sand, I show you how do it. It's all those goose, he jus' come step out on sand, jus' walk like soldier, long string. Ol' Coon jus' take off belt, his lit'l drum, an sed it: 'Well, my fren's, you jus' make it big ring, I stay in middel. I sing an beat it drum. When I stop sing an play drum, all you gooses jus' shut eyes tight an dance slow jus' like what I showed you now. Then Ol' Coon he's jus' dance nice to show 'em how, all those goose. He say, Ol' Coon: 'You musn't stop dance 'till I begin sing 'gen, an jus' keep shut all time, yo' eye. It's how they dance eva'body, down that place I jus' come now.'

"So all that gooses jus' make ring, like he's tol' em Ol' Coon, an all jus' shut his eye an list n while he's sing good, Ol' Coon, an jus' beat it that drum. He's jus' sing:

'Ho-he-yah, ho-ha,
Yah-dra-wah, ho-ye-yah,
Ho-ha, yah-dra-wah.'

"Then when Ol' Coon, he quit singin', all those old goose jus' dance 'roun' slow an easy like, all his eye jus' shut. Now Ol' Coon jus' reach out queek, an grab one ol' fat she-goose, jus' snap his head off 'fore he could squawk, an thro' it behin' him in hurry. Then he's sing agen, an when he's stop sing, those goose jus' dance 'roun' slow like, an he grab 'notha one, fat one, an queek, twis' head off an throw behin' him, then he do same thing, an get 'notha one. But jus' when he's ketch 'em las one, lit'l ol' she-goose dancin', open one eye jus' lit'l bit, cause he want see if he ain't bes' dancer. That she-goose when he see what he's do that Ol' Coon, jus' holler loud an sed: 'Oh, he's kill us! An all those goose he's fly way, like big hurry.

"Ol' Coon he's jus' laff, an pick 'em up his three goose an lit'l drum, an start on to his lodge. He's think he's got good suppa' now.

"While he's goin' long, he's say to he-self: 'I b'lieve I like 'em betta roas' gooses.' So when he's come his lodge, he's fix his gooses, an pick up lots of stick to mck big fire, cause by-um-by it's burn all down an meks good lots coal an ashes, good place to roas' 'em gooses. It's good suppa' he's got now, by-um-by, soon.

"It's w-a-y down long river, Ol' Fox, his lodge. By-um-by he's look out an see big light, big fire on hill clos by his lodge, Ol' Coon. Ol' Fox he look, an he say to he-self: 'I wonda' he's come home, that ol' rascal, an what fo' he's got big fire. I jus' slip 'roun' that way an see what he's do.' So he's call his little nephew what's live with him, an tolc 'im don't need to mck fire in lodge, cause he's goin' 'way an not come back 'til late. It's what he sed, Ol' Fox, an tell 'em nephew: 'You go sleep.'

"Well, 'bout that time, his fire, Ol' Coon, it's all burn down, an make good ashes an hot coal. He's take stick an scrape all 'way that hot coal, an lay 'em down that gooses on his back, all, one, two, three, in row, his foot all stick up straight out ashes jus' like beans what's jus' come up in garden.

"It's gettin dark now, an wind it's blow. He could hear 'im up in limbs on tree. Ol' Coon, up high on rocky hill, he's set down by fire an jus' lis'n. He's kin' tired that Ol' Coon, an it's jus' soun' easy that wind, an make 'im feel sleepy-like. He's lis'n to riva' down there, too, jus' soun's good, an by-um-by he's jus' sleepy-like eva'thin'g. So, he say to he-self: 'I could take it nap while it's cook, my suppa', I do that 'cause nothin' botha' it 'tall.'

"It's some limbs way up high ova' he head, jus' makin' noise 'cause wind it's blow and jus' mek squeek when it's rub togetha' that limbs. Ol' Cool' he's sed: 'Hey, you noisy fellas up tha',' I want sleep lit'l nap, you woke me if it's botha' anythin' 'bout my suppa'.' He's say a right that limbs, an by-um-by that Ol' Coon he's curl up an sleep good, jus' lit'l ways from fire."

III

Old Coon Sleeps Too Long

A stick of wood in the fireplace burned in two, and the sparks went flying up the chimney's black throat. The Boy took the poker and drew the other logs closer together. Meanwhile the tall old clock struck off eight resounding peals, finishing with its usual whirr.

"Neh-ah, it only said eight, can't you go on and tell me if that poor Old Coon, hungry as he was, got to eat his fine supper; or did it all burn up while he was taking such a good nap. He made such a great fire, I'm wondering."

After turning to the boy's mother, who was sitting near by sewing, and addressing a few words to her in Wyandot, the Old Aunt said:

"No, it don burn it up, his suppa'. Spec he don bin so mad if it did. He no bizness lay there an go sleep it so good; but he's jus' all a time such a smart, it's jus' good 'nough fo' him. I tole you lit'l mo 'bout it, then you go bed.

"Well, it's a ready come up, big moon, down th'a in east; but it's jus' sleepin' yet, Ol' Coon, don wake 'im up, nothin'. By-um-by, up there in rocks, 'bove where it's sleepin,' Ol' Coon, you could see 'em sharp nose an sharp eyes too, jus' 'roun' edge of rock, lookin' down where's sleep, Or Coon. Then when see he's sleep good, that Coon, Ol' Fox he's come down, jus' walkin easy, he don't step on rocks, no nothin', jus' walk sof' an don mek it noise. He's look all 'roun' that Fox, an by-um-by he's see 'em that six goose foots stickin out row in ashes.

"'Ah-e-e-e,' he jus' sed it easy, 'that's reason he's got big fire, Ol' Coon. I glad I'm fin it, an I glad I'm come see 'bout it that big fire. I lik' 'em roas' gooses, an I could jus' 'bout eat 'em three of it. He's good one, hunta, my Couzzen; but must a-be it's heap tired now. Too tired, can't eat em; well, I eat 'em that goose.'

"He's look at that Ol' Coon all a time, but he's jus' sleepin' good now, so Fox he's jus' step 'roun' easy an get stick, an scrape way ashes from that gooses. It's roas' nice, an jus' smell good. It's some limbs up there in trees jus' sque-e-k, but it don' botha' him, Ol' Coon.

"Fox, he's get busy eat it that goose an by-um-by it's jus' nothin' lef' but pile bones—it's got lots meat on yet, cause he's jus' eat it bes' part, that Fox. He's got nuff fo' he's eat all of it; jus' can't eat no mo'. It's jus' sque-e-k all a time that limbs, but don wake it up nothin' that Ol' Coon.

"When he's eat all he want, that Fox, he pick up all-a bones an put em back in ashes, an he's cova' all up 'gen jus' lik it's don botha' it nothin'; an he's stick in row gen, all that goose foots in ashes, jus' same lik he's fix it, Ol' Coon.

"It's lit'l pile sof' ashes clos' by, an he's go there, Ol' Fox, an he's jus' dance all ova' it, so's he could fin it his tracks, that Ol' Coon when he's wake up. He sed it: 'I think my Couzzen he bin glad I come see 'im, he bin glad I don woke 'im up, cause he's heap tired.'

"He's jus' fix it eva'thin' that Fox, then he's go downhill towa'ds riva'. It's fine night, moonlight, an he's jus' walk long riva' bank 'til he's feel kinda tired and sleepy-like that's cause he's eat so much goose. By-um-by he's come to big one tree what's stan way out ova' riva'. It's look like good place to sleep, so he's clim' up an fin' good place to stretch out, an by-um by he's go sleep. Big moon, it's yellow, shine jus' ova' that Fox, down through limbs what don' got no leaf on it, and mek good shadow that Fox down in clear wata'; it's jus' lik' he's down tha' in wata', that Fox.

"Well, by-um-by up on hill, that Ol' Coon he's jus' wake up in hurry an he's sed: 'I guess I take good nap, mebbe.' An he's jus' stretch he-self an look 'roun'. He's jus' think: 'Well, I got good suppa' anyhow, must-a-be cook good now.'

"He's go in hurry ova' to fire an reach out bofe hands an ketch holt goose foots to lif' it out of ashes. He's jus' lif' kinda hard, lik' it's heavy, an he's jus' tumble back an roll ova' holdin' that goose foots in his hand. He's jus' feel lik' funny, an he say: 'I guess it's cook too much, my suppa'.'

"He's get up an go ova' there fire 'gen, an take it out that otha' goose foots one at time. He's don' know what's mattah, an he's jus' look lik' funny eva' time he's take it out that goose foots; then he's take stick an scrape way that ashes, an don' fin nothin' jus' pile bones with lit'l bit meat on it. He's jus' much mad, an he's sed it:

"'He's jus' bin here, some lazy thief an steal it my supper. I jus' like to seen it, I bet I bust 'im his nose. I jus' like to fin' out who done it, I bet I poun it good. Must-a-be it's that Ol' Fox, he's the one. He's jus' think he's get even fo that crawfishin' I tol' 'im how to do it. At jus' joke, that one. It's m-e-a-n trick, this one. It's a right for him, jus' wait I ketch im, I poun' 'im an lick 'im good, I don' care fo' hund'ed snakes, how much he's holler, when I fin' 'im.' He's jus' get madda' all time that Ol' Coon, an he's jus' shake his fist at those limb up in trees, an sed: 'What fo' you don' do it like I sed it, wake me up when I sleep it? I tole you that way, ain't it?' He's jus' pickin' meat off those bone, while he's scold it that limbs, an he's jus' mad like eva'thin'g. He's jus' scold som' mo' that limb, and sed it:

"'What fo' you don' keep still now, you don' have to mek noise, you jus' mek me mad all a time. If don' stop you mekin noise, I come up tha' when I finish pick this bones, an I mek you stop.' That limb he's jus' keep on squeek, sqe-e-e-k, all a time, an it's so mad that Ol' Coon jus' hurry and eat that bones, so he could go up an whip it those limb.

"When he's get thro' eatin' that bone, he jus' look 'roun' and by-um-by he's fin' it that place where he's dance, Ol' Fox. Ol' Coon he's fin' it that tracks, an when he's look at it, he's jus' m-a-d, some mo. An he's jus' pick on that limbs som' mo', an sed it: 'I jus' come up tha' an I fix it you fellas.' So he's jus' go up that trees til he's come to that place where that limb it's kin' a broke, an it's in fork, an wind it's blow an jus' make it that noise where it's rub. Ol' Coon, he's jus' take hold that big limb with bofe han's an he's jus' goin' throw down. He's so mad he don see that mebbe so might pinch 'im that limbs, cause it's jus' swing. Fust he's know it jus' ketch 'im his hand, that limb, an just pinch 'im tight. Oh, it's hurt like eva'thing. He's jus' pull an pull, that Coon, an jus' make worse. By-um-by he's pull it out; but it's hurt b-a-d his hand. He's sure get hard time, that Ol' Coon. He's jus' slip off try to sleep mebbe."

IV

OLD FOX MEETS HIS COUSIN

It had been snowing, and outside a keen, sharp north wind was rioting everywhere. The Boy, having finished his evening chores, came in with some hickory logs for the fireplace.

The fire-light alone lit up the room, and the old brass andirons glinted in its glow. Neh-ah was sitting in her usual place, and the Boy, taking his, said:

"Neh-ah, this is a fine evening for some more stories about Old Fox and Old Coon. I know it is so cold outside that no snakes or grasshoppers or anything else will hear you telling them."

"Yooht! What fo' you don' get tired hear 'em ol' story? Jus' seem like you want it all a time, ol' story. Guess you betta go you Uncle Jim, Canada, cause he could tole you that kin' Injun story, all kin' 'til you get tired to lis'n. Long go when we all young folks, we go down Gram'ma Hunt, his house, winta' time, an jus' lis'n to ol' story, lots of em. Was bes' one to tell 'em story, Gram'ma Hunt. Neva' did get tired to lis'n, an he's jus' lik it to tole us that kin too. Only was some kin story jus' fo' ol' folks, he don' tole to us that ones.

"What 'bout I tole you las' time? Oh, yes, Ol' Coon he's los it his good gooses suppa', an Ol' Fox he's bin fill up plenty.

"Well, seems like when Ol' Coon so mad an mek that big talk 'bout how he's lick 'im that Fox, he's heard 'im sed it, that Mista' Skunk; so that Skunk, he's jus' go right now an tole 'im 'bout it that Fox what he's sed it that Coon, how he's goin' lick 'im. Then he mad, that Fox, and he tell 'im Skunk: 'You jus' see, I lick that Coon, myself, fust time I seen it.'

"He don had no chance fo' few day tho', cause that Coon he's jus' stay at home, cause it's bad sore, his hand.

"One night, it's kin a late, that Coon he's think, 'I guess I go ketch 'em crawfish.' So he's go down by riva' an ketch 'em good many, take 'em his lodge an have good suppa'. He don' take it no naps this time.

"When he's done his suppa' he's jus' think, 'I take lit'l walk cause don bin nowhere, long time.' So he's start out long riva' bank. Eva' thing jus' seem like good to that Ol' Coon, he's jus' trot 'long sing low like to he-self. He's jus' like happy, an jus' keep on goin'. By-um-by he's get sleep like, an jus' wish he's back his lodge; but it's long ways, so he sed it: 'I fin some place take nap. Right that time he's come long clos by that big tree. What he's seen it Ol' Fox. Jus grow leanin ova' wata'. Ol' Coon, he's think it good place, so he's clim' up in lit'l fork limb. He's jus' fix good 'bout go sleep, an he's hear somethin'.

"It's big moon yet, an jus' bright. Ol' Coon he's look down riva'bank an he's see it comin Ol' Fox, jus' trot 'long trail. He's jus' keep still, Ol' Coon, like he's sleep; but he's look straight down unda' him an he's see his shadow in wata', looks jus' like him. He's look at that Ol' Fox an he's lookin' at that shadow, too. He's jus' lookin' m-a-d, an Ol' Coon he's hear him sed it, Ol' Fox: 'Here it is that Coon, in wata' lookin' fo' crawfish now. I jus' slip up an jump on im give im lickin. So, Fox he's jus' slip up edge riva'bank, eye jus' snappin'. He jus' mek big jump down in wata' where he think it that Coon. He jus' make it b-i-g splash, an prit' soon come up top wata' an he's jus' sputtah an blow b-i-g, jus' like almos choke 'im. Then he's hear that Coon up in tree jus' laff l-o-u-d, an say: 'Hey, Couzzen, it's early to swim, ain't it? I hear Gran'fatha Turtle he sed it, you mustn't jump when you don' look, an you mustn't be too hurry.'

"That Fox he's crawl out on bank an he's jus' sheever. He don' sed nothin', jus' commence pick up stick an brushes an pile it foot of tree, lit'l ways clos' to mek fire. He's put l-o-t-s stick an mek it big fire, an when it's burn good, he's jus' sit down foot that tree, that Fox, jus' like he stay there till he's come down tree, that Coon.

"Prit' soon, Coon he's sed it: 'My Couzzen, sure you not goin' set tha' long time. You coat lots wet, mebbe so ketch 'em bad cold. I glad to come down talk to you, mebbe so gif some my tobacco to smoke, cause must-a-be wet yours afta' you jump in riva'. I spec I stay here tho, it best one, cause I could see good up this tree. Mebbe so somebody comin long to botha' you, I seen it an tole you 'bout it.'

"Ol' Fox he don sed nothin', jus' set by fire, back up gainst tree, an jus' keep it shut, his mouth. It's hard work tho', that kin'. That Coon he could drop in wata' an get way; but he jus' think he's stay in tree an talk an foolish 'im his couzzen.

"By-um-by, he sed it: 'Well, I sleep it lit'l bit now.' So, he's curl up an sleep it.

"Afta' long time he's woke up. It's shine bright, big moon, way high. He's look down an its settin' by tree yet, that Fox, jus' soun' sleep it. Coon he's jus' slip down e-a-s-y, 'til he's clos' to that Fox. He sleep it good, could heard 'im snore. Coon, he's jump easy down on groun'. He don move nothin' that Fox, sure nough sleep it. He's bad one, that Ol' Coon, he's jus' take it long one, stick, dry leaf on end, an he's tickle it his nose, that Fox; but he's so sleep don botha' him nothin'.

"That bad one, Ol' Coon, he sed it to he-self: 'It prit' good chance, mebbe so I make it 'notha' tricks on my couzzen.'

"So, he's jus' slip long down by riva'bank where he fin' it lots sticky mud, it's red. He's get big one, chunk, that muds an jus' spread on flat rock, an put it on wata', jus' stir lit'l bit an make it heap sticky, just like what you call it, moh-lass. Then he's took it that muds an jus' rub all ova' his face, that Fox, put lots that muds on his eye. He's jus' step back lit'l bit, that Coon, an look at him, that Fox, an he's jus' laff good to he-self, an sed it: 'My poor couzzen sure have good time to wash it face in mornin', if it's dry good that muds. I spec' I start home now, mebbe so it's time.'

"Well, he's started that Ol' Coon an go lit'l piece, then he's jus' rol'l ova' on groun' an jus' laff big at that Fox 'till he's tired.

"It's 'bout gone that moon, jus' comin' daylight in east, when he's woke up that Fox. What's matta'? He's woked up sure; but can't see nothin', can't open it his eye, not jus' lit'l bit. He's jus' stagger an run into stump an bush, jus' fall down, almos' tumble in riva'. It be good thing he did, cause soak it up that muds; but he don' done it.

"He's jus' rub it that dried muds but he don' come off, an eye jus' stick 'em tight shut, can't open. He's sure bad fix this time, an jus' m-a-d like dickens. Jus sed it all a bad name could think of 'bout that Ol' Coon, jus' cuss him heap, I guess. It's don' do no good that kin' tho'.

"Well, he try to find path go to his lodge, but jus' get tangle up in briar-patch, an it's stuck 'im all ova'. It's b-a-d lucks fo' him that Fox, sure. He jus' don know what do nex'. So, he's jus' set still lit'l bit, study what do. Prit' soon he's hear, tap, tap, tap, on dead limb 'way up high his head. He's lis'n 'gen an heard it, tap, tap, tap.

"'Yoh-ho, my fren',' he's sed it, 'come here, got big trouble me, mebbe so you could he'p it.'

"It's come fly down hurry, that lit'l speckle woodpecker bird, an sed it; 'What's mattah, my fren', what I can do he'p it you now?'

"Fox he say: 'I like to have you tried it, pickin' this dry muds off my eye, so's I could see how open it my eye.'

"'Mebbe so, it's too much sharp my bill,' it's sed it that woodpecker bird. 'I pick 'em prit' hard, but I see what I do, I don' hurt you, I can he'p it.' So it's go to work, woodpecker bird, jus' set on end his nose, that Fox, an pick 'em e-e-a-s-y as can, but it's sure make im come blood, cause it's sh-a-r-p that woodpecker bird, his bill. Well, that Fox he could see how open it his eye, prit' soon an jus' looks good to him, eva'thin'g. That lit'l bird tell im to washin' his face good in riva'.

"That Ol' Fox, he's feelin kin a good 'gen, an jus' thank it that woodpecker bird, an sed it: 'What I can do fo you, my fren', cause you sure do big he'p' with me?'

"That lit'l woodpecker bird he sed it: 'Oh, my fren', long time I jus' wish I could had it on my head, lit'l spot, red jus' l-e-e-t'l one spot, not big one like he's got, Great Woodpecker, Quankquank-queh.'

"Fox he's sed it: 'That's good, my fren', I fix it that lit'l spot, red one.' So he's took it's 'some blood on his face where it's drop down, an he's pain't it lit'l spot, red one, on his head, that lit'l she woodpecker bird. It's jus' stay there, too, that spot, eva' since.

"Oh, he's so glad that lit'l she woodpecker bird, jus' fly up in tree an try his bes' sing, but can't do it much. Well, he's got it red spot anyway, an jus' lots happy.

"That Fox, he's jus' trot off on trail long riva' an try to think what could do get even with him, that Coon."

V

Old Coon Visits the Sugar Bush

The Father had been mending a crack in one of the Mother's treasured old maplewood bowls, made more than a century ago by a Wyandot, when the tribe lived in Canada, along the beautiful Detroit.

The Boy having watched the work of pouring the melted lead into the broken place in the bowl, turned to his aunt and said:

"Neh-ah, you and I will make sugar this year. We'll tap the trees down along the bluff, and have some real maple syrup. We can take our lunch everyday and have a sure enough camp. You can tell me stories while we boil down the sap."

Nch-ah nodded assent and replied:

"Yes, that jus' like you, always think some way to get story. Anyhow, I don' tole you yet, what he's do nex' Ol' Fox an Coon, an what you talk 'bout minds me of it. He's always mek it maple-suga' Ouendots. It's lots a work, too, but he don care fo that. Could jus' keep im busy do somethin' all a time. Don had no clock, no ah-man-ac them days, tell em how much time gone. I spec don get ol' so quick, peoples them days."

"Well, days bin get lit'l long, sun he's start go back north. It's time come bright night an frosty mornin', an kin a warm sunshine daytime. It's jus' 'bout time go suga'-bush, those people, tap tree an mek em maple-suga'. Jus make lots of it, put in mo-cocks, use in winta' time. It's *kin* a hard works mek em suga' them days, cause got to mek em lots trough birch-bark, ketch'em sap. He's got b-i-g trough too, mek em out a big log. Don had no kettle them days; jus' have to put em hot rock in big trough; but he don care fo nothin' them peoples, don care fo hundred snakes, cause he's jus' got lots a times, them days. Don got no times do nothin' now days.

"Jus' 'bout this time year, he's jus' like it to follow them peoples to suga'-bush, that Coon. He's alway jus' like it, poke 'roun' in suga'-camp, come night, an he's sleep it them peoples. That Ol' Coon he's jus' l-i-k-e it to put it his nose in trough an drink it lit'l bit sap, s-w-e-e-t one. He like it good that sap, an sometime if he don found it in lit'l trough, he's try to get one drink out a that b-i-g trough. It's hard to do that one tho, cause mebbe it's prit' hot that sap in big trough, an it's always jus' keep cover up that big trough with nice boa'ds, white ones, jus' mek it out a lin-wood, them peoples.

"Afta' he's put it on that Fox that dry muds, it's long time no seen each otha that Fox an that Coon. He jus' thought it Ol' Coon, it's prit' near even to him, that Fox; an mebbe so he won't try nothin' 'notha kin tricks. He don want see im tho, an jus' keep out a way, cause he might try mek 'notha tricks on im, that Fox. It's jus' go on that way fo days, an Ol' Coon jus' 'bout think: Well, I guess mebbe so he's fo'get it, that las' trick, my couzzen.

"But that Fox, he don fo'get it nothin', no seh. He's prit' sharp, *an* he jus' all a time got it, that what you call em—'watch-full-a-waitin'. He's know it Ol' Fox, 'bout his couzzen all a time likes to foolish 'roun' that suga'-bush, when that peoples he's mekin suga', an he's know it how he like it to drink that sap, heap s-w-e-e-t. So, he's just keep it, his 'watch-full-a-waitin', an when Skunk tole im: 'Ole Coon not home, bin gone three-fou' days,' that Fox jus' sed it: 'I spec' mebbe so it's gone suga'-bush, my couzzen, I guess I go see.'

"Well, he's start that Fox to go suga'-bush. It's fine days an when gets there, jus' see all a peoples heap busy, work. Fox he's jus' slip 'roun' edge ov camp, all a time he's lookin' fo sign ov that Coon. He's look l-o-n-g time, *an* by-um-by he's fin' tracks long edge lit'l branch, that Coon he's bin lookin' crawfishes, mebbe so.

"It's late in evenin', while he's sleep it some place that Coon, Ol' Fox he's jus' get busy. Afta that peoples he's gone to all lit'l ones, trough, to get it, sap, Fox he's come 'long behin, an he's jus' turn it, bottom up, eva' one that lit'l trough. Then he's go look in big trough. It's prit' near full sap, it's hot.

"So he's sne-e-k 'roun' some mo' an watch it good Ol' Squaw cover it big trough, all good with that white boa'd. He's jus' watch it 'roun' till it's all fix it, eva'thing, an them peoples it's all sleep it. Then that Fox he's slip up by big trough, an jus' push it two that boa'ds, lit'l ways part.

"Well, he's jus' push it ova' them two boa'ds 'til end of it right on edges ov big trough. It's smell good that sap, prit' near mak' em Fox want some he-self; but he don botha' it, 'fraid might ketch im his own trap, I spec'. When he's all done fix it, that Fox, he's jus' go lit'l ways, hide in bushes an watch for him, that Coon. He's wait long time, an by-um-by he's hear it comin somebody, jus' grumblin to he-self. It's that Ol' Coon, an Fox he's hear him sed it: 'Wonda what fo so steengy, them peoples; jus' turn em upside bottom all lit'l trough. Can't fin' lit'l bit sap. Mebbe I could get drink on big trough if don turn it upside bottom, too.'

"Ol' Fox he's keep it still, jus' kin' a chuckle tho', cause he knows goin' ketch im that trap what he fix it fo Ol' Coon.

"That Coon jus' come pokin' long slow like, till he fin it that big trough. He's jus' walk all 'roun' kin' a easy, jus' sniffin an lookin' fo crack. Fox he's fix it chunk right front where he's fix it that boa'ds, an that Ol' Coon he's jump on that chunk, his nose stick up in air, an jus' get good whiff that saps. It's kin a hot. Well, he's set on chunk lit'l bit an jus' lookin' roun'. He don't seen nothin', then he's jus' mek 'notha' jump an he's lan' right on end ov that boa'ds what's he push it ova' that Fox. That boa'ds he jus' slide ova' otha' way queek, an that Ol' Coon he's jus' go kerplum in that hot saps.

"Them boa'ds make big rattle noise an it's wake im up that Ol' Squaw. He's come out lodge see what's matta' an come by that big trough jus' time he's crawl out Ol' Coon. He's got big stick in his han' that squaw, an jus' hit that Coon good whack on side when he's run way. He's jus' go hurry, Ol' Coon, an by-um-by when he's go thro' bush, somebody sed it: 'Hoh, Couzzen, you like it to take good wash in hot sap, ain't it? Mebbe so ain't good 'nough wata'?'"

VI

Old Fox and Old Coon Both Try a New Venture

Neh-ah, you said there was one more story about Old Fox and Old Coon and that it was a long one, too. Now, this evening while everyone else is gone and just you and I are sitting by the fire, won't you tell it to me? I'll go down cellar and get some of those apples we like so well, and we'll have a regular party."

After his return with the apples, an after putting some hickory logs on the fire, the Boy seated himself in his accustomed place and waited for the story.

"I wonda' what's goin' do when it's all gone, story. If you bin live long time 'go, ol' man they took you, an jus' mek story tella out o' you, so you could tell em all a young mans when you get be ol' man. Nowdays jus' have book an noose-paypa' an eva'thing an write down. It's seem funny to Injun first time he know that kin, jus' think white man mek paypa talk. Mebbe so you could write it somethin' story, someday, then won't have tell em, just could read it anybody.

"Las' time, that Ol' Coon jus' bin fool' 'roun' suga'-camp, ain't it? Good fo nothin' jus' spoil it all big trough sap fo that poor ol' Injun woman. Anyhow, 'bout that time, spring jus' begin think 'bout turnin ova'.

"Them days jus' get some mo' long. South wind, he's come now an mek it all broke up ice in riva' an jus' go float 'way. It's kin' a blue smoky all 'roun' an you could smell it that brush an leaf it's bin burnin', caus' it's garden patch clean up them peoples. Buds on tree it's swell up an no mo' peoples in suga'-bush, all gone back to village. Prit' soon plant corn patch, when leaf on hick'ry tree 'bout big as squirrel, his ear.

"That Coon don see it, Ol' Fox, since time Ol' Coon he's fall in big trough. Somebody sed it he's gone mek visit with fren' way down end of lake, Ol' Fox.

"Coon, he's jus' study all a time how get even on that Fox fo las' trick he's bin play. Jus' think all kinds, cause he's want make em bes trick yet on that Fox, cause he's prit' mad to him yet.

"Well, South Wind he's drive it all 'way that snow and ices, even that patches long north side hills. Early mornin' you could heard it lots wild gooses and cluck. Jus' go, 'honk, honk,' like what you call it—auto'bile, when jus' go long road like dickens, an seen somethin', in road, nowdays. That goose an ducks he's comin' back from south, an he's jus' stop ova', visit few days all long. Could fin it lots good eat in marsh long riva', jus' fore it's run in lake.

"Ol' Coon an eva'body jus' glad to see come back, an jus' holla' to him somethin' when he's fly ova. He's all a time glad ketch em two-three, too, if he could do it, foolish em or somehow.

"One day, sun mo than half ova', Ol' Coon he's start out try to ketch em goose. It's lots of em down marsh, an he's want try new way ketch em. He's jus' slippin long e-a-s-y like, riva'bank, an he's meet im Lit'l Fox, it's his nephew, Ol' Fox. He's live with im, his uncle, an he's treat im mean, all a time, that uncle. Jus' mek im work hard, that po' lit'l nephew, an feed im nothin' 'cep' scraps. Eva'body know that kind, an jus' feel sorrow fo it, cause that uncle jus' whip it an mean to it all a time. He's prit' near starve, you could count it his rib, an jus' few hair on it, his tail. Seem like, all a time, he's goin' dodge somethin' that lit'l fella.

"His garden patch, Ol' Fox, it's good one, beans, pumpkin, eva'thing all good; cause that nephew an his aunt jus' work it plenty. Ol' Fox, he don't work lit'l bit, but he's jus' all a time brag it that garden patch, an he's always tole it that nephew: 'Took care of it my garden patches.'

"Well, that time when he's met im Ol' Coon, that Lit'l Fox, he's look like he feel prit' good, that lit'l fella, an he's tole it to Ol' Coon, his uncle bin gone on visit way down lake. Ol' Coon he's always feel sorrow for im, that lit'l fella, an jus' all a time be good to him. Jus take him go hunt, an showed it an tole it lots a things 'bout how to hunt. He's tole im tho' musn't tell im you uncle, cause it jus' mek im mean to lit'l fella some mo. So, when he' seen im that time, Ol' Coon, he's sed it: 'Well, Lit'l fella, my couzzen, what you look fo this time, is it come home you uncle?'

"Lit'l Fox he's say: 'Mebbe so he's come back tomorro' mornin'. Mr. Skunk he's tole him las' night, my aunt, when he's stop lit'l bit our lodge. We bin all clean up garden patches, an I jus' think I go hunt it some game.' Ol' Coon sed it: 'Well, young fella,' jus' stayed by me. I got good way, new one, try to ketch em gooses, mek em good one dinner, bofe of us, mebbe.' Lit'l fella, he sed it: 'Uncle, you all a time mek good one, hunt, good one ketch em, all a time kill em ten, I spec' so we ketch em heap this time.'

"So, they jus' trot 'long togetha' an Ol' Coon jus' 'splain 'bout that new way ketch em gooses. He's goin' fin' it lit'l bunch gooses what's bin eat plenty, an jus' swiminin' 'roun', prit' clos' to sho'. Cause if he belly full, he don't hink 'bout nothin' botha' im, he's sed it, that Coon. He's got long rope, lit'l one, what he's made out sof' bark. It's stout one, too, an he's tie on it that rope, three-fou' slip-knot. When he's fin' it lit'l bunch gooses, he's goin' dive in wata' an swim unda' where's that gooses, an put it that slip-knots ova' his foots, many as he wants them gooses. Jus' jerk em queek an swim to bank an pull em in them goose.

"Well, afta' whiles they fin' it lit'l bunch ov gooses, an that Coon he's tried that new way ketch em. Prit' soon he's got three ov it, jus' like he sed it. It's su'ah good ketch em that way. They jus' go on some mo an by-um-by seen it 'notha lit'l bunches goose. He's swim it close to bank. Ol' Coon he sed it: 'Lit'l Couzzen, you like tried it this time? It's good chance. So, lit'l fella he's take that string an he's go afta' it that gooses, an prit' soon he's swim to bank jus' pullin three fat goose. He's jus' feel b-i-g, that lit'l fella, an Ol' Coon he's jus' glad fo him too.

"So then, start home an Ol' Coon sed it: 'Tomorro' go gen, lit'l fella, cause won't stay long now them goose, jus' go north. I come by you lodge when sun jus' pass middel, an we go ketch em some mo lots a gooses mebbe.'

"Nex day Ol' Coon he's go down by that place what he sed it; but he ain't there, Lit'l Fox. He's wonda' what's matta lit'l fella, don come. He's look prit' soon an seen it that lit'l fella jus' workin' hard in that garden patches. Coon he's jus' whistle low like, an that lit'l fella he's heard it an he's come down there where is it Ol' Coon.

"Coon, he's sed it: 'Well, what's matta? Le's go ketch em gooses 'gen.' That lit'l fella's he's jus' look sorrow, an he's tell it, Ol' Coon, can't go, cause his uncle, it's come home. He say his uncle ask im how he's ketch it that gooses, an when he tole him, he sed it why don ketch em mo, he sed it his uncle: 'I could eat all of it that many myself.' Lit'l fella sed it, 'I tole im go 'gen today, but uncle jus' say, he go he-self,' an tole him lit'l fella get long rope, stout one, bes' he could find, cause he's goin' try ketch em gooses, he-self. So lit'l fella say he got im good rope fo his uncle, an that uncle he jus' went down to'wa'ds lake to tried it his lucks. He tole him, lit'l fella to stayed home an clear out 'notha garden patches. That Lit'l Fox he's jus' look sorrow, an that Coon he's lis'n to him, an jus' thinkin lit'l bit.

"By-um-by they jus' heard it way down by lake, b-i-g squawk noise, an lots a honk, honk, soun like lots a auto'biles, I guess, jus' soun funny like holla' lots a gooses. Jus bofe stop talk an lis'n. Seems like comin' close by, so that Coon an lit'l fella jus' run top lit'l hill, it's close by, where could see betta down on lake. It's look that way, an could seen it b-i-g bunch gooses, jus' fly eva' which way an down low, jus' make lots a squawkin' an honk-honk noises. That Coon an lit'l fella jus' look at each otha', like say, what's matta? Prit soon it's kin a strat'en out that bunch a goose, jus' fly mo high up, an then start out fly comin this way. When it's come lit'l close, looks like they could seen it' somethin' hang down, jus' swingin' like, unda' that bunch a gooses. Jus comin close now, 'bout fly right ova' where it is that Coon an Lit'l Fox. Then they seen it, what 'tis; it's that Ol' Fox. That rope it's tie tight on his middel, an it got lots goose foots tie on it too. He's jus' swingin, looks like ridin good. When he's go by close, he's jus' holla' l-o-u-d, that Ol' Fox an sed it: 'Nephew, took good care my garden patches,' an jus' keep right on ridin f-a-s-t.

"Ol' Coon, he's try it not to smile an he's say: 'Well, Lit'l Fella, I guess mebbe so, he tied it too much goose foots on his string, you uncle, he's got prit' good string seem like. It's new way travel, but I spec he go long ways an fin it new place, mebbe so. I spec not come back, long time, mebbe so betta go some tell him, you aunt.'

"That Ol' Fox he prit' smart, afta' all, I spec mebbe so he's first one ride on airyplane, ain't it?"

VII

A Pre-Historic Race

Neh-ah, in the last story, Old Fox was certainly 'right up to date,' wasn't he? He had an aeroplane with a motor that couldn't go dead on him, and besides, he had a honk-honk that could scare everything out of the way. Now that there aren't anymore stories about Old Fox and Old Coon, I wonder what you are going to tell me next. I'll read you some more of the *Arabian Nights* and you can think up some others."

"Well, that good, but spec betta tole you 'notha one tonight, cause jus' bin think 'bout it today, when you tole to me 'bout it that airship race, you read in noose-paypa. That one mind me 'bout it, and jus' think it all ova' this afta'noon while I'm piecin' quilt.

"It's 'bout one o' you great-gran'fathas I spec', 'cause you b'long to Big Turtle clan, jus' same as me and you motha', an our motha', cause all a childrens have to b'long same clan as motha'. Long 'go, always bin lots a good chief an warrior in Big Turtle clan. He's leader long go, way back, don know how many hun'ed years. Lots ol' story tole 'bout it. Big Turtle he's hol' the world on his back fo long time. Someday I tole you 'bout it.

"That Ol' Turtle, he's the one, he smart all a time. He jus' same since long time go, all a time know it what do. He can't scared him nobody, an can't beat im nothin'. He's eva' time come out head.

"That why, long time go, Ol' Buffalo, he's eatin 'roun' clos' edge of timber. He don't hungry, he's jus' bite ova' here, ova' tha'. By-um-by he see Ol' Fox in bushes, he sed it: 'Yo-ho, my fren', come ova' here, I like tell you this.'

"Ol' Fox he's lit'l smart too; he's crawl out trap e-a-s-y; he's hard to fin' it, too, sometime you hunt fo him. He's jus' wonda' what's want Ol' Buffalo, an what's got say; but he's come ova' tha, jus' jumpin easy an he's sed it: 'Well, my big fren', what you got say?'

"Ol' Buffalo, he says: 'My frien', I got make race with Turtle. You kin' a smart, an you got sharp eyes, you be judge, see who beat em. You tell him, Ol' Turtle, I beat im on a ground or in a wata', jus' how he like, I don care nothin'. You tell im come tomorro' ova' there by lake when sun come up jus' 'bout high as sycamo' tree. You tell eva'body an he can come see race. I be down tha', you tell im that, Ol' Turtle. He's always best one, eva' time; but I don't think he could run, it's too short his legs. Mebbe so he's run good in wata', tho. Me too, I could run fas' in wata' or anyhow. I bet I could beat im.'

"Ol' Fox he say: 'I tell im Ol' Turtle an I tell im eva'body. I go now.' So he's go down by his lodge, Ol' Turtle, an tell im all what he sed it, Ol' Buffalo.

"That Turtle, he's jus' lis'n an don say somethin' for long time. By-um-by he say: 'That's good, I run race on wata'. First one come to that islan' ova' there, he's the one what beat. You tell im, Ol' Buffalo, I be on han'. I don say jus' what I'm do, but I do im. Tomorro, when sun shine good, I come.'

"Fox, he's go back tell im, Ol' Buffalo, what say Ol' Turtle. All what he see on way, he tell em 'bout race. He sed it: 'You tell em eva'body, you tell em come.

"Nex' day, ain't sun-up yet, Ol' Wolf he's go down by lake. He's make it fire, make smoke jus' go straight up, so can see eva'body, an by-um-by, all come.

"Prit' soon he's come along, Ol' Turtle; jus' come slow an go down clos to edge wata'. He don say nothin', jus' go slow, lookin' 'roun'. Buffalo an Fox come too, an bofe jus' talkin all a time. Then come eva'body, Deer an Bear, Coon, he come too. Turkey, Prai'chicken, Duck, an Quail, Hawk he's tha too, an Little Turtle, Snipe, an Ol' Beaver, Porkypine, Snake, an Mud-Turtle; it's come eva'body I guess.

"While all jus' talk an visit 'roun', Buffalo he's go down where Ol' Turtle he's settin close to edge wata', he sed it: 'Well, my fren', you legs prit' short, but I beat you this race, I think.' Turtle he don say nothin', jus' lookin' cross lake to islan'. Buffalo sed it: 'You say we race on wata', I tell my fren' Fox be judge. It's high rock right ova' there, so Fox he's clim up an set down, an he could jus' seen it, eva'thin.'

"Buffalo sed it: 'Well, it's re'dy. Wolf, you howl it, an hit it three times queek on drum, an we start. Wolf, he say, 'Al'right,' an he took he place. Prit' soon he's howl, an hit it three times on drum queek; they gone. Buffalo he's swim fast to'ads islan'. Turtle he jus' slip in wata', an can't see him, nobody. He's go jus' like that wa'boat you tell it 'bout on otha side Big Wata; that Gemmany Keeza' summarine, unda' wata', an when Buffalo jus' lit'l mo an halfway, swimmin fas', Ol' Turtle jus' crawl out slow on sho' of islan'. Eva'body looks funny, and Fox he's say: 'Turtle he's beat im.'

"Beaver he's try it an Turtle he's beats im. Nex' Deer he try; he's way behin' an Turtle crawl out on islan'. Coon he's sed it: 'I sure can beat im, I re'dy now.' He's jus' got start, when Turtle crawl out on otha' side. Well, then Turkey say: 'I want beat im. He can't do nothin'.' Turtle he's right on islan' when Turkey he's come. Prai'chicken he say: 'I'm good racer, I could beat im;' but Turtle got tired waitin' for him on islan' befo' Prai'chicken got tha' an start back. Quail, he's whist'l big, an sed it: 'I'm the one could beat im Turtle.' Turtle neva' sed nothin', jus' get re'dy. They start an befo' eva'body don heard Quail, his wings any mo, Ol' Turtle he's crawl out on islan'.

"Fox, he's got tired sayin' Turtle's beat im; so he said it: 'You can't do it, nobody. You can't beat im, Turtle. He's good racer in wata' cause he's all a time good swimma. All what's got beat, mus' gif to him' somethin'.'

"Well, all them fellas what's got beat, Buffalo, Deer, Bear, Raccoon, Turkey, Prai'chicken, an Quail, they jus' cut it off lit'l bit they own meat. They gif' to him, Turtle, jus' one piece to time. Turtle he's took it each lit'l bit when they gif' to him; don sed nothin', jus' eat all of it.

"Then Fox he's sed it somethin', 'gen: 'Long as he live that Turtle, it be jus' same; if them peoples kill im an roasted it or make em soup, it's tasted jus' like all a kinds game meats. Turtle, he's take it first place, at head all kin's animal. He wise an brave, an he don all a time talk, he's do somethin'.'

"Turtle, he don sed nothin'. Jus ten' his own business, don't buck in nowhere. Don botha' nobody. It was that way.

"But Turtle he's don tell it them peoples that Ol' Turtle, his brothah, look jus' like im, live on that islan'.'"

VIII

THE EAGLE FEATHER

That race you told me about was a good story, Neh-ah, anyway that's what I think. Can't you think of another one about Old Turtle to go with it?"

"It's jus' all a time that way. I tole you one an you jus' want it 'notha one kin a like it. Someday it's goin' be all gone, story, what goin' do then?"

"Oh, let's don't think about that. I know you've got a whole lot of them yet, and if you do run out, why I'll just ask for some of the best ones, and you can tell them again. I never get tired of listening to any of them."

"Yooht—you jus' like that Ol' Turtle, he jus' get the best of im eva'body. Don botha' him nothin' an he's just all a time go on an 'ten to his own bizness. He don worry 'bout it somethin' he's jus' think it out some way eva'time to come out head, an he's do it too. I spec' that's why he's good leader, cause he jus' all a time lis'n, an lookin' an thinkin fo hese'f.

"Well, I tele you 'bout eagle featha'. It's bes' kind like em, Injun. Long time go, can't wear it eva'body; womans, he don wear 't all, an young buck he couldn't wore it till he's do something big. Ol' time it's that way. Nowdays, jus' stick im in his hat, eagle featha' all a Injun, an anybody. Jus' same like that iron crosses what he's gif' to all he so'jers, that Gemmenny Keeza', you read me 'bout em in paypa.

"It's this way he's get it, eagle featha', first time, Injun. It's long go, jus' commence worl' I spec'. It's ol' man an he nephew live togetha, jus' them two, it's all a people, them days. Ol' man he's jus' stay in lodge all a time. Young fella he's go out get it, game, hunt. Well, one time come back lodge, don't get it nothin'. Uncle he's ask im what got, an young fella sed it: 'Nothin'.' Next day it's same way, an jus' same way, 'notha times. It's three time, then when come back, young fella, an his uncle sed it 'gen, that young fella sed it: 'I pull it out eagle featha',' an sure 'nough, he's got it that featha' in his hand. Ol' man he's jus' shook it, his head an sed it: 'Oh, it's a big danger.'

"So he's tole young fella hang it that featha' in smoke hole, top of lodge. He's do it, an prit' soon they seen it that eagle fly slow like, ova' that smoke hole. He don got that featha' tho'.

"Ol' man, he's sed it 'gen: 'That's a big danger, must call animals to Council. Musn't let get it, Eagle, that featha'. So young fella he's go tell em come to Council, 'bout that danger. By-um-by they all come; Big Turtle, Otter, Skunk, Porkypine, an all of em. Ol' man tell em, 'We musn't let Eagle an his fellas take it way from us that featha'.' He's pick out his crowd to hol' it that featha'. All them animal jus' talk heap 'bout what he can do. Some run fas', some could hide good, an some could jus' make it big noise to scared it anything. Ol' man he's tol' Deer don't want im, cause can't run fas' 'nough. He don want Wolf, he's too much howl, an Bear cause he's too much all a time sleep it.

"He's pick it out Big Turtle, Porkypine, an some mo fo he side. Prit' soon they seen it, Eagle jus' fly low ova' smoke hole, 'gen. Some them fellas what he don take it, Ol' Man fo his side, jus' get mad to him, an sed it: 'We goin' he'p it, Eagle.'

"Turtle, he's slip 'roun' an got it that featha', an tole it his men: 'Le's go.' They start off lit'l ways an come to big tree. Turtle sed it: 'Le s clim' up.' So all of em clim' tree. They look way off an seen it comin' Eagle. Jus 'bout that time it's come big wind. It's rotten that tree, an jus' broke it an fall down. They jus' go eva' which way, all them fellas. Porkypine, he's all cover up with rotten wood, but he's chawed it way an crawl out. Mebbe so that's why he's all a time like to chawed it rotten woods, Porkypine. An he's kin' a hurt too, lit'l bit, Porkypine, so, when Turtle say: 'Le's go, hurry,' Porkypine say he can't travel. Then he's tole im Turtle, 'Get on my back,' an he's give him basket ashes to scatta' on his tracks, that Turtle, so can't fin' trail, nobody, them otha fellas.

"He's got it that featha', Turtle. Well it's started all of em. Turtle, Porkypine on he back, they las' one. Porkypine he's jus' get it busy scatta' ashes on Turtle, his tracks; but shucks, it don't hide em track't 'all, jus' make easy to see it trail.

"They jus' go on hurry, an'way, an it's prit' nea' get to riva', when he's heard em comin, Eagle an his bunch. Jus 'bout edge of wata, Turtle, they jus' holla', 'Who-o!' an jump out an ketch em that Turtle, Eagle, his bunch. They try to take it 'way Turtle, that featha'; but can't do it. Turtle got it in he mouth an can't let it go, an won't give up, that Turtle, e'tha'.

"So he sed it, them fellas: 'We fix it, Ol' Turtle.' An one of it jus' mek it fire an when it's burn good, they jus' pick im up Turtle an carry im bottom side up top, an jus' hol' him ova' fire. Ol' Turtle sed it: 'Oh that such a nice, I jus' like it that kind, plenty hot, don't took me out a fire my fren's, I like it.' Them fellas jus' mad an sed it: 'It don't hurt im fire, le's took im out, whip im. So they take it out fire, an some fellas get good sticks an jus' beat im, Turtle, on his back. Turtle jus' commence sing, jus' like it was beatin' drum, them fellas, an jus' seem like a happy. He's made some mo' them fellas, an Turtle he's got it yet that featha'.

"Somebody sed it: 'Le's throw im in riva'.' So they pick him up an start do that. That Turtle he's jus' scream, an sed it he's 'fraid a wata' an jus' beg 'em not put im in riva'. He's jus' push back an holla' an don't want go 'tall, jus' mek 'em big fuss. Them fellas jus' glad then to heard im, an sed it: 'We jus' throw it in deepes' wata' we could find.' An sure 'nough they jus' pitch im that Turtle, 'way out in deep wata', ka-zowey. They could seen him sink down bottom of riva' an layin' on his back, like dead, but he's got that featha', yet.

"Well, them otha' fellas think its dead, Turtle; but prit' soon they seen im swim out 'cross riva' an clim' up on big log, an he's jus' wave that eagle featha' an jus' give big wah-whoops.

"So, them fellas hold council, an they sed it: 'Somebody mus' go get it, that featha'; but don't want go nobody, cause 'fraid of wata'.' By-um-by talk some mo', an send it, Otter. He's swim out that log quick, an Turtle, he's jus' set there an hol' it up that featha'. 'bout time Otter he's get there, an goin' crawl on that log, Turtle, he's drop in wata' on otha' side log. He's go unda' log prit' quick on otha' side, 'gen, an he's bite on end Otter his tail. Then jus' go 'roun' an 'roun' that log Otter an Turtle. That Otter he's jus' holla'; 'Ow-we-e, he's hurt me, ow-we-e!' Prit' soon that Turtle, he's bite off piece tail an Otter, he's get 'way, hurry, an swim to sho.'

"Turtle, he's get on log 'gen an wave that eagle featha' an jus' whoop 'em heap.

"They couldn't beat im nobody, that Turtle, that's cause he's bes' one yet."

IX

WHY AUTUMN LEAVES ARE RED

A Wyandot Myth

It had been a clear winter's day, not cold and with just enough bright sunshine on the first light snow that had fallen. The boy had been out in the woods with his dog; and down in a sheltered place along the bluffs, he found some dog-wood shoots yet bearing their brilliantly colored leaves. Gathering some of these he had brought them home and placed them in an old silver flagon that stood on the mantelpiece. They made a wonderful bit of bright, cheery color in the room.

Of course he called his Aunt's attention to them, for he well knew how much she liked bits of bright color.

He saw her look thoughtfully at their scarlet and crimson and was all interested, yet not surprised when she said:

"Ol' Ouendots use's tell story 'bout how come leaves get prit' color in fall times. Not long one, story, but jus' kin a nice. Cou'se it's 'bout some animals, cause seems like long time go they was live first, 'fo' peoples. They somethin' like peoples, too, I guess, cause they do so much things all a same like.

"Didn't I ever tol' you what's reason it's red an color, all tree leafs in fall time?

"Well, it's like this one: Long 'go when it's all fix it up, Sky-land, by Little Turtle, Deer, he's got in hurry an went up tha' 'fore it's all fix it fo animals. It's jus' mek em mad, all of em, cause that Deer he's all a time such hurry to buck in.

"Afta' while when it's all ready eva'thing, Bear, it's his time to go up tha', so he's go up by that nice road what he's fix it, Little Turtle, an when he's got up tha' prit' soon, he's meet im, Deer. He's sed to him: 'What fo you come here so hurry, fo he's tol' you, Little Turtle, it's ready?' Deer, he's awfu' proud like an he's jus' shook his head, an sed it: 'Nobody but Wolf could ask that to me, he's the one to sed it, not you.' An by-um-by, he's sed it, 'notha 'gen: 'I'll jus' give you whippin', Bear, cause you such a smart,' an that Deer his eyes jus' like fire, an hair on his back, jus' stan up straight cause he's mad.

"Bear, cause can 'fraid him nothin', he's jus' stan tha' waitin' fo that Deer to jump on him, I spec

"Then Deer start it. Bear jus' growl big, mek loud noise, jus' like shake sky, an he sharp claw jus' tear that Deer, an Deer, his sharp horn an foot, jus' cut that Bear. They fight long time an mek big noise. They could heard it them otha's down on Great Island. Then they sent him up that Wolf to stop it that fight.

"Wolf, he's get up tha' an he's got hard time to mek stop it that big fight, that Deer an Bear; but he's do it prit' soon, an when that Deer, he's run way his horn jus' all drippin with blood, that Bear's. That blood jus' fall down on tree leafs on Great Island, an mek it all red color. It's that way yet, ev' time come 'roun' that time they fight it, that Deer an that Bear, leafs jus' get that way, red.

"They sed it long go, Ol' Ouendots."

X

The Ferryman

When this story was finished, the old clock hadn't yet, as Neh-ah sometimes remarked: "He's sed it, eight."

The Boy was ready with another suggestion, and said: "Now Neh-ah, you've told me such a good story about the red leaves, I think you'll have to tell another about a rabbit. Old Jolly and I brought home seven. You'd hardly believe it, but Jolly run one into a b-i-g hol'low red-oak that stands down on the hill-side. Someone had cut a hole in one side of it and I crawled in; and down in the old hol'low roots running all 'roun'd, I kept pulling out rabbits until I had seven. Mebbe we won't have a pot-pie, and I'll sell some of them in town, too."

Neh-ah listened smilingly to the Boy, then said: "Well, guess can't cross riva' no mo nobody, cause must be you kill all the ferrymans. You don't give im no good chance or mebbe so they foolish you like he done to one fella, one time.

"I didn't tell you befo' 'bout Rabbit, is it? He's live long time go down on riva', an he's got good canoe, an jus' took em eva'body cross riva', like what you call it ferry-boat, ain't it?

"Well, one time Rabbit, he's sittin down on riva'bank, jus' singin an waitin' like, an prit' soon he's holla' somebody, otha' side of riva'. Rabbit, he's look and seen it, of Wolf, so he's jus' don mek no tention, jus' keep on singin like don't heard nothin'. That Wolf, he's mean one, all a time want kill em somebody, an Rabbit he don't like em.

"Prit' soon Wolf sed it: 'Hey, you fella you feet it's crooked out, come took me cross riva'.'

"Rabbit, he's jus' ke'p on singin, an by-um-by he's say: 'Long go, I all a time dance plenty at feast, 'at's why it's crooked out, my foots.'

"Wolf sed it: 'Hey, you fella, at's got l-o-n-g ears, jus' stick it up straight, come took me cross riva'.'

"Rabbit, he say: 'My ears stick it up, cause long go I could wear many eagle featha', ain't it?'

"Wolf, he sed it: 'Hey, you fella, it's split you lip, come take a me ova' riva'.'

"Rabbit, he say: 'It's that way my lip, cause long go, I whistle much at big dance, ain't it?'

"Wolf, he's jus' mad now, and sed it: 'Oh, you jus' brag heap, all a time, I get you now. Then he's jus' jump in riva' an swim cross. Rabbit he's run an Wolf he's took afta' him. He's run long ways an jus' gettin tired, but Wolf, he's comin, he's prit' close now. Rabbit, he's come to hollow tree, an he's jump in hole, jus' time Wolf he's goin' ketch im.

"Wolf, he's mad, an he jus' goin' stand by that hole till that Rabbit, he's come out, n'en he ketch em sure, so he's stay right tha'. Rabbit he's rest lit'l time, n'en he's go out 'notha hole an go back to his canoe. L-o-n-g time afta' Wolf, he's get heap tired that what you call it, watch-ful-a-waitin', an he's go back down riva'. He's look otha side an seen it that Rabbit sit on his canoe, jus' like bin tha' all a time.

"That's time he don ketch im Rabbit, that Ol' Wolf, ain't it?"

XI

OLD COON TEACHES THE WOLF TO HUNT

Neh-ah and the Boy were sitting just in the fire-light one night when the old woman said:

"You jus' always like it to hear em so much story 'bout Ol' Fox an Ol' Coon, I jus' happen today, think of 'notha one kin a like it. 'Tain't Ol' Fox tho', cause he's gone an I don eva' hear if he's come back. Mebbe so if you heard it someday 'bout his come back, you could tell that story. But that Ol' Coon he jus' always took eva' chance what come long to play trick on somebody.

"Anyhow, I tole you this story jus' same way you Uncl' Jim Clark use' tole it long go in Canada. He was good one to tole story, only sometime he jus' put in lots a cuss words like he all a time sed it white-mans. Them Injun boy long time go at s jus' first thing learn Inglis', it's the cuss words. I guess it's cause in Injun langwige they don got none, cuss words.

"It's long time afta' he's gone that Fox, one day Ol' Wolf he's prowlin' long riva' an he's meet im that Coon. Ol' Coon he's bin on visit way out west to pra'rie peoples, an he's bring it home big bundl' buffalo meat. He's jus' eatin piece when he's come long Ol' Wolf.

"Wolf he's sed it: 'Hello, my Couzzen, what kin meats you eat em, an where you get it? I don had no good meats fo long time, it's kin a sca'ce now days, ain't it?'

"Ol' Coon he's jus' kin a grin, an gif' to him piece of meat, that Wolf, an he's sed it: 'Oh, it's a buffalo meats what I got. I ketch em that kin buffalo out on pra'rie, where I bin few day. It's lots of it there, buffalo, an it's kin easy to ketch em that kin too.'"

"Wolf, he's jus' eatin an it's sure taste good that meats. Prit' soon he's say: 'How you sed it's easy to ketch it that kin? He's big one than you are, an could run fas'. I don see how you mek it easy to ketch em that kin.'

"'Well,' Coon sed it, 'I could tole you how it's easy ketch em, you wants to tried it. He's big one, but he's easy to 'fraid, an when he's heap 'fraid, he's jus' scare to death, jus' run til it's kill himsel'.'

"Wolf he's say: 'You ketch im that way?'

"'Yes, I ketch im,' he sed it Coon. 'I jus' tole you all 'bout it an you could tried it an ketch em good, then you have lots a good meats. You could start fo prai'rie prit' soon an come to edge, long 'bout dark come, jus' befo'. You jus' look 'roun' good an fin' it bunch buffalo, eat 'roun' close to bushes. You watch em n' afta' whiles its tired eat it, an it's lay down sleep it. When he's good lay down sleep it, you jus' go long easy, slip up behin' an you jus' tied it, that buffalo, his tail 'roun' yousel', you middel. It's long hair on his tail, that fella. You mus' tied it good, so can't slip off, cause if slip off, he's turn 'roun' jus' step on you, sure. When get it tie up good, you jus' mek big noise—whoo, whoo. Buffalo he's so scare he's jump up an run, an you jus' took good ride, cause you jus' go with im, an jus' all a time go whoo, whoo. That buffalo he jus' run heap, he's so scare, an prit' soon he's jus' drop dead, then you mus' cut it, his throat, an you got heap good eat.'

"Wolf, he's jus' lis'n, an he's sed it:

"'It's soun' good, I guess mebbe so, I tried it. Le's go, you jus' watch a me, I kill em buffalo.'

"So Coon he's go long, an they start it for pra'rie. It's 'bout dark when they gets to edge of timber, an right clos by seen it bunch buffalo. Wolf an Coon jus' lay down rest lit'l bit, an watch it that buffalo. Afta' while it's got nuff eat it, an jus' all laid down to sleep it.

"Wolf, he's jus' feelin prit' good an he's pick it out big fat, she one buffalo. Well, when he's sleep it good that ol' she one, buffalo, Coon tell him betta go now, an he's slip out easy an he's tied he-self good to that she one, buffalo, his tail, an when it's all tie up tight, Wolf, he's jus' go holler: 'Whoo, whoo.' That she one, buffalo, he's 'fraid plenty. He jus' jump up an holler: 'Bra-a-h, bra-a-h,' an jus' go run, he so scare, jus' like what's say white peoples: 'scare like hell.' He sure run fas' an that Wolf he's jus' hoi tight on his tail, that she one, buffalo, an jus' ride fas' too. Eva' once while, buffalo jus' kick im in ribs an Ol' Wolf he's go up in air. Prit' soon he's gone out a sight, buffalo an wol'f. Ol' Coon he's jus' kin a chuckle an sed it to he-self: 'I guess mebbe so, my couzzen, he's get prit' good ride, now, won't get back fo many moons, mebbe so, spec he's go 'long ways.'

"But that Wolf, he don ride such long time, cause that she one, buffalo, he's come to big mud hole, wide one, an jus' 'bout time he's get middel that mud hole, he's mekbig kick an that Wolf, he's break it loose from tail, jus' go up in air, an come down tchi-wash in that sof' muds. He's kin a glad too, cause don want it no buffalo meats now. He's crawl out mud hole kin slow, cause prit' sore, an start off kin a limp, an he sed it to he-self: 'That Coon he's don say how long got to ride it, that buffalo. I guess he's jus' mek it foolish with me. Nex' time I don't tried it what he say.'

"It's jus' same kin he's always foolish im that Ol' Fox. He's bad rascal that Coon."

XII

The Hole in the Sky or How the Summer Became Longer

W ell, I guess that Old Coon never did stop playing his pranks. I only wish that more of his tricks had been told in other stories, for it is sure fun to listen to them." So the Boy said one evening when he was not quite sure that Neh-ah had another story for him. He was right pleasantly surprised when she at once said:

"I goin' tell you 'notha one Uncle Jim's Story. Ol' Tah-too-tahn-yoh, he's ol' Jibway man what's marry to Ouendot woman, an live 'mongst our people in Canada, long go. Lots a boys jus' go down his house winta' time an he's tell em ol' story, sometimes prit' near all night. They jus' pitch in an cut it lots wood fo ol' man an he's tell em ol' story. It's good story, this one, I like it myse'f.

"Long time go, ol' people use tole 'bout it, it's jus' col' all a time, prit' near. I think mebbe so, it's that time, f'ain't very ol' world, cause it's them days, peoples and animals, jus' kin a all same like, sometimes they be peoples, sometimes some kin animal, jus' what kin they like. They know how to do eva'thing them days, got power, jus' like what call white peoples now, witch, I guess, anyhow, could do jus' what want do, anything.

"Well, it's them days, good hunta, he's lodge not far from Big Watah; but it's no body live clos' by, jus' him an woman, an got one boy, lit'l fella, jus' 'bout half way grown to man. It's big country, lots tree, big ones all run where he's live, that hunta. He's got strong power, could prit' near do it anything. Sometime he's man, an sometime he's that lit'l kin animal what dey call it, Fisher, jus' kin a like that Otter, 'at's his Couzzen, an kin a looks like im, but he ain't that big. That Ol' Otter, he's kin a funny fella, he's jus' all a time, laff an sing, an have good fun. He's all a time talk heap, too; but he don sed nothin' much, jus' talk. He's good fella, tho', an jus' try to do it anything what tell im, somebody.

"That hunta he's all a time kill em heap deer, an eva' kin a game, so, jus' have plenty to eat. That woman, he's good one, too, jus' take care that game what he's kill em, dried that deer meat an smoke im, an mek that fine buck-skin fo moccasin an leggins.

"They jus' like im, heap, that lit'l fella too. That hunta he's mek im good lit'l bow an arrows, an showed im how hunt bird an squirrels; an that woman, he's mek em lit'l moccasins an leggin' an huntin' shirt. Snow shoes too, cause it's jus' plenty snow that country all a time. It's that way them days, jus' col' an snow prit' near all time.

"That lit'l fella he's jus' go hunt by himse'f an bring em back to lodge, bird an squirrels; but he's jus' get prit' near freeze it eva' time. His finger jus' 'bout freeze it, an can't shoot good, an sometime jus' mek im mad, an jus' cried, cause it'so cold, don know what do. He's jus' wish it don be so much freeze it an cold fo so many days.

"Well, one time, that lit'l fella, he's bin hunt, an jus' comin' back to lodge. Oh, it's col', an that lit'l fella, he's 'bout froze it now. He's comin' long, an he's seen it, squirrel, it's sit on bush lit'l way head, it's eatin' somthin'. He's wonda' that lit'l fella why don run, squirrel, an he's jus' fix it his arrow to shoot it, 'bout that time, that squirrel, he sed it:

"'Grandson, musn't shoot it, me. Put it down you bow cause I got somethin' to sed to you. You jus' lis'n an you do what I sed it. Long time I seen it you don't like it heap col' an snow, I seen you huntin' an jus' can't help it, cry sometime, cause heap col'. It's too plenty col' all a time, anyhow, I don like it too. Now I tole you what do, an we fix it mo summa' time. You fatha', he's strong power, he could do it prit' near anything. When you get you lodge, you mus' jus' cryin' all a time. Yo' motha', he's want know what's matta', you jus' don sed nothin', jus' cryin', an cryin' heap. Jus' keep it cryin' all a time 'til he's come, you fatha'; then when he's ask it what's matta' don sed nothin' fo long time, but jus' cryin' an cryin' jus' likes feel so bad, can't sed nothin'. Then afta' whiles, you tell im': 'Me, I don't like it too much col' all a time, I jus' want mo summa' times.' Just sed it: 'Oh, my fatha' can't you have him, somebody, make it mo summa' times, an don have it so much col' an snows. Oh, I don like it so much col'.'"

"So, that lit'l fella, he tole im, squirrel, he do that way, an he's got to lodge, he's jus' cryin' an cryin', jus' like it hurt somthin but don know what. He motha' ask it what's matta', but jus' shook head an don't sed it nothin', jus' push way what's want im to eat it, his motha', an jus' keep cryin' 'til it's come his fatha', then he's do jus' like what's tole im that squirrel.

"Well, he fatha' sed it: 'My son, I try do that what you sed it. It's much hard thing to do, but I tried, cause my son want it that kin.' So that lit'l fella he's stop it cryin' an eat it what gif' to im his motha'. That

Fisher sed it, he mus' make feast an call council for his fren's. Nex' day they cook it whole bear, an sen' word to Otter, Beaver, Lynx an Badger to come that feast an council. Well, afta' whiles, it's come eva'body an had it big eats; then all a them fella jus' sit 'roun'd an prit' soon smoke it peace-pipe, then jus' talk 'bout it, what's got do.

"Afta' talk 'bout it long time, all them otha fellas sed it they go with that Fisher an he'p im. He sed it, they go in three days. Time come that Fisher he tole it goodbye, that woman, an lit'l fella, an he's jus' feel heap bad, cause he's know mebbe so he don seen it no mo.

"Then he's start all of it, an jus' go on, don't meet im nothin' til 'bout twenty days, it's come to foot of high mountain. Jus could look up as want to, an can't see it top, it's h-i-g-h, that mountain. They fin' it tracks, like kill it somethin', somebody, jus' while go; you could see bloody, an that track goin' up mountain. That Fisher he sed it, betta follow it that track, mebbe so fin' it somethin' eat it. So, jus' followed it, track, an prit' soon, come to lodge. Fisher, he tole em, mus' be still, don laugh fall.

"By-um-by, they saw ol' man stan in door that lodge. He's jus' crooked eva' which way, jus' all twist up. He's got b-i-g head, an funny kin' teeth, jus' all stick out an he don't had no arms. Them fella's they wonda' how he could kill em anything. That ol' man he's ask em come in his lodge, cause it's jus' 'bout night, come.

"That ol' man, he's strong Monedo, he could do anything. Well, afta' whiles ol' man he's bring out big bowl meat, an he's jus' gif to them fellas some fo their suppa'. He's jus' move 'roun' heap funny, an that Otter, he jus' can't he'p it, an prit' soon he's laugh. That Monedo, he's jus' look at im, an jus' jump on him goin' smother im, cause it's that way he's kill it anything. But that Otter, when he's felt ol' crooked man light on he's head, he's jus' slip out from unda' im an he's jus' run out door an get way; but that Monedo he's sed it bad fo im that Otter.

"Rest of em they eat, an smoke an talk, prit' near all night. That ol' man he's tole Fisher he could do what's he's want do; but it's a hard one to do, an mebbe so, it's kill im. He's tole im which way to go, an sed it fo them to do like he said it, an if follow that road, it sure take em right place. Whe' he's tole em all 'bout jus' what to do it, eva'body sleep it lit'l time.

"Come nex' mornin', started go on. Jus' gone lit'l ways an meet it tha' Otter, he's 'bout freeze it, an kin a hungry; but that Fisher, he's took long some that meat what's gif to im that ol' crooked man, so that Otter he's eat it. He don laff this time.

"Well jus' travel eva' day till it's 'bout twenty days gen, an they come to that place what's tell em 'bout, that Monedo. It's the highest mountain, yet. Have to clim' long ways fo'get to top, but they get up tha' an jus' sit down rest and smoke it, peace-pipe, cause got to do that kin ask em Great Spirit, he'p em. Jus' put it tobacco in that pipe, an hol' it up to sky, then to no'th, an east, an south, an west, then to earth then smoke it. It's so high up that mountain, that looks like sky right tha', an think, an look all 'roun' fo long time, an afta' whiles, that Fisher, he sed it, 'We mus get ready,' an he's tell em, 'We got to mek hole in sky.' He's tole it that Otter try it first. Jus' jump up 'gainst it hard as you can, mebbe so break it hole. Otter, he's jus' kin a laff, an sed it, 'I tried it, mebbe so.' He's jus' jump hard, jus' hit that sky so hard it's jus' bounce im back, an prit' near knock stuffin' out that Otter. He's fall on snow right on he's back, an it's kin slick that snow, an that Ol' Otter he's jus' go slidin like eva'thing, clear to bottom that mountain. I bet he's neva' travel that fas' gen. When he's come to bottom, he's shake he-se, an sed it, 'I think mebbe so, I gone home, I don like make it that jump 'notha 'gen,' so he's jus' pull it out fo home.

"Well, that Beaver, he's tried it, an it's fall down all a sense knock it out that fella.

Then Lynx, he's tried it an it's jus' all a f-a-r, an it's plenty grass, plenty tree; same kin, jus' laid tha' like's dead.

"'Now,' he sed it, Fisher, to Badger, 'you tried it, it's strong, you people an could do heap.'

"Badger he's jus' tried hard, an it's knock im back that sky, but don hurt im, so, he's jus' jump up an he's tried it 'notha 'gen. This time, its look's kin a like it's crack, that sky, so Badger, he's jus' puff up b-i-g, an he's jump, like a white peoples sed it: 'jus' like a hell.' It's bust hole in sky an Badger he's go through an that Fisher, he's jus' jump in right afta' im.

"Them two fellas jus' look 'roun' an oh, it's fin' place, jus' like a prai'e, could see plenty all kin's flower. Jus lit'l stream run eva' which way, lots a birds jus' ever kin prit' ones jus' singin' eva' direction, oh it's jus' like a nice eva' where. Right ova' tha' they seen it some good ones lodges an way ova' good ways off could seen it lots a peoples jus' playin' ball, havin' good time.

"Don't seen nobody in them lodges but could see lots mo-cocks an baskets an it's all jus' full all kin birds, prit' ones. That Fisher he's jus' think of that lit'l fella an they jus' cut it open them mo-cocks an baskets all they could an let it out all those kin birds an all of it jus' go big bunch an fly down that hole in sky what's made it Badger. An all that warm weather what's 'roun' tha' it's go down that hole too, an jus' spread out all 'roun'. Prit' soon them peoples way ova' tha' they see it them fellas what's doin' an jus' come run ova' that way; but time they get ova' tha' it's 'bout all gone through that hole, all a summa' time weather, jus' 'bout lef' nothin' 'cep' its tail, an one fella he's come runnin, an he's hit it with big club, an jus' broke it off tail; summa' time 'bout to went through that hole.

"That Badger, when he's seen em comin' them fellas he's jus' run fo that hole but that Fisher, he's jus' keep on lettin out lots mo bird fo that lit'l fella, an he's stay too long, that hole it's growed up an can't get through. Well, he's jus' strike out runnin' cause to get way from them otha' fellas, an he's run fas'. Prit' soon he's come to tall tree an he's clim' up. They come, them fellas, an shoot at im, arrows; but that fella you couldn't hurt im if you hit im, jus' one place arrow could hurt im, jus' 'bout one inch end of he's tail. Prit' soon one arrow hit im on that place. It's prit' bad. He's look down tha' an seen it one them fellas, he's got totem same like what he's got. So, he's holla' to him, this fella, an he's tole im, 'You my couzzen, tell em don kill me.' When dark come them fellas quit shoot, an that Fisher, he's come down, he's feel prit' bad, cause it's bleed heap. So he's start crawl long to north, mebbe so he fin' hole in sky he can go through; but he's jus' keep travel 'til he's 'bout give out, don fin' none. So, he's stretch out his legs, his head to no'th, an sed it: 'Well, I did that what's want, lit'l fella. It's make it betta' fo all of its peoples, have mo summa' times now, maybe eight o' nine moons, summa' time, then he's jus' die. Them fellas fin' it nex' day, stretch it out dead. You could see it in sky now, it's tha' yet. While peoples call it that stars, Big Bear.'"

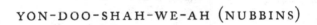

YON-DOO-SHAH-WE-AH (NUBBINS)

"O-See-O"[2]

To those who claim by heritage and blood
The undisputed, inviolate right
To call themselves the True Americans;
Whose ancestors were of whatever tribe,
Of Choctaw, Cherokee, or Wyandot,
Miami, Ottawa, or Ojibwa,
Or Shawnee, Seneca, Modoc, or Creek,
Quapaw, Sioux, Cheyenne, Peoria;
To all of these, and to all other tribes,
I dedicate the poems written here.

Hen-Toh
Wyandotte Reserve,
Ottawa County,
Oklahoma.

2. "O-See-O," a Cherokee word of greeting.

"Yon-Doo-Shah-We-Ah"[3]

"Yon-doo-shah-we-ah!"
'At's how they sed it,
Wyandot, nub-bins;
It's little fellas,
 Corn, his ears.

Ol' times, ol' womans
Braid 'em long string corns,
White an red an blue,
Hang it high in lodge
 Fo' winta' times.

"Yon-doo-shah-we-ah,"
Don' braid, don' hang high;
Jus' throw it one side
An braid 'em nice corns,
 To hang it high.

But when he's done braid
All them fine big ear,
He's take it nub-bins,
He's shell 'em, an made
 Oh, good hominy!

---

3. "Yon-doo-shah-we-ah," Wyandot word meaning nubbins. Pronounce each syllable just as it is spelled; or rather just as each would be pronounced in English, with a slight accent on "doo" and a more marked accent on "we."—Hen-toh

The Calumet

Sent from the white lands of the North,
Emblem of peace and brotherhood,
Its first fruits ever are offered
To The Great Spirit, then to the Sun;
To our Mother, the Earth; and the Waters;
To the North, to the South, the East, the West;

Then to each other.

A prayer goes to the One Great Spirit, thus;
Oh that the whole wide World could now
Accept the Redman's ancient symbol,
Off'ring its incense to the Universe;
And blot out fierce, wild war's red stain,
Bringing Good-will to earth again
    With Peace, white Peace.

1918

My Fren'

To J. W. C.
On his leaving for the Army during the great war

You my fren', no diff'ence what say, anyone,

If I seen you now, or don' see fo' years.
You know reason, t'ain't what I done,
You could look my eye, don' seen it tears,
    When you sed it: 'Good-bye.'

You my pardner, you sed it one time,
It's l-o-n-g 'go, but me, I don' fo'get;
If you go flat bust, an I got one dime,
I know wha' you could fin' nickel, I bet,
    Or mebbe ten cent.

It's jus' that way all time, me an you,
We bin know'd each otha' how you say, well.
I don' care fo' hundred snakes what you do;
Even you tell it me: "You go to hell,"
    I could do it, e-a-s-y.

You come back war-trail, it's be jus' same,
Kin' a smile and sed it: "You my pardner yet?"

I jus' look at you an sed it you name,
Mebbe so wink it, then sed it: "You bet!"
    I don' fo'gotten nothin'.

Injun Summa'

You seen it that smoky, hazy, my frien',
It's hangin' all 'round' on edges of sky?
In moon of failin' leaves, 'at's when
It's always come, an jus' floatin' by.

You know, my fren', what's make it that kin'?
It's spirits o' home-sick warriors come;
An somewha's his lodge fires all in line
Jus' near as could get it to his ol home.

I think he's like it, Happy Huntin' Ground,
It's mus' ta be a nice, eva'thin' ova' tha';
But, mebbe so, fo' little' bit, jus' kin' a look 'round'
When year it's get ol', an days an sky it's fair,

He's kin' a like to wanda' back ol' huntin' ground.

But don't want a stay. No, cause it's all gone,
Beaver, Bear, Buffalo, all; it's can't be foun';
Anyhow, makes good dream fo' him, 'bout eva' one.

So he's come back an make it his lodge fire,
All 'round' ova' tha' on edges of sky;
An it's nice wa'm sun, an you don' get tire,
Cause it's Ol' Injun Summa' time, 'at's why.

The Seasons

What sed it Ol' Injuns 'bout a spring time?

    Oh it's prit'ty girl, it's comin' from a south,
    All dress' up in fine white buckskins.
        He don' walk, he's jus' dance,
        He don' look, he's jus' glance
        'Roun' at eva'body, pleasant,
            Jus' like happy;
An he's bring it nice bowl o' strawberry,
        An jus' scatta' eva'wha'.

What sed it Ol' Injuns 'bout a summa' time?
    Oh it's good woman followed that girl,
An it's dress like a nice, jus' all kin' a green.
        He don' dance, jus' kin' a float,
        Like on wata', seen it, boat,
        An jus' smile 'round' eva'-wha' goes,
            Jus' like good;
An he's bring it' string o' squaw-corn,
        An jus' pile up eva' wha'.

What sed it Ol' Injuns 'bout a fall time?
    Oh it's young man comes from kin' o' west,
Huntin' shirt an leggin' kin' o' color brown.
        He's straight jus' like an arrow,
        An his fringes color, 'yarrow.'
        He's got laugh in eye an it's a keen,
            Jus' like brave;
An he's bring it bunch o' wil' grape an acorn,
        An jus' hang up eva' wha'.

What sed it Ol' Injuns 'bout a winta' time?
    Wooh! It's o-l' man, he's comin' from a north,
From Ian of Great White Rabbit, 'at's his home.
        His long robe it's shine an glis'en,
        You could heard it clink, you lis'en,

When he's walk kin' o' slow
   Jus' like tired.
He's bring lots o' ice an plenty snow,
   An jus' drift up eva' wha'.

Fishin'

Eva' fishin' much? It's good.
Sunshine in sky, shade in a wood,
Down on riva' bank jus' wait an wish
I could ketch 'im hurry, that dam fish;
    Take 'im home, cook 'im, an eat 'im.

Sometimes it's ketch 'im right now,
Sometimes don' ketch 'im all day;
But Injun he's sure know how
He could ketch 'im a'right, 'notha way.

Long 'go 'fore whiteman, he's come here,

Ol' Injun use to fishin' with spear.
That kin' o' spear it's made o' stone;
He's got hook too, made o' bone;
    But he could ketch 'em plenty fish—sometime.

Sometime he's fishin' on a shore,
Sometime he's fishin' in canoe;
Some day he's ketch 'em plenty more,
Some day it's jus' nothin' do.

Now days he's got littl' stick, green an red,
L-o-n-g line, he's wind it up, 'at's how he sed.
It's tie on end littl' fish made o' wood,
Lot's o' hook, seems to me it's no good;
    But he's sure ketch 'im b-i-g one, bass.

That bass he's like Injun, mebbe so,
Whiteman's fool' 'im easy, since long 'go.
Spec' so, dam fool', bofe of it,
Cause you can't fool' 'im, whiteman, littl' bit.

HEN-TOH

FIRE

I think Injun like it betta' 'an anythin', fire,
    But I don' jus' know why.
Mebbe so it's cause 'at smokes go high,
    Way up towa'ds a sky,
An could carried it message, higher an higher,
    'Til He's got it, Great Spirit.
When he's smoke it, Peace-Pipe, any-wha'
    Council, or in lodge,
Smokes curl 'round' jus' kin' a like it's dodge
    An gatha' up eva' body's message,
An carried it off, jus' way up tha',
    'Til He's heard it, Great Spirit.

Long 'go, sometime, he's want it sen' word
    His fren's way off, 'notha' wha.
He's fin' it high place, an tha'
    Make it smokes go straight in air,
An his fren's, it's like they heard,
    What he's ask Him, Great Spirit.

An Injun, his folks, time come when he die,
    He's bury him somewha', not far,
An on grave, 'bout time it's shine star,
    He's make it littl' fire. What for?
It's make it light fo' soul on road, 'at's why,
    To place wha' He's call 'im,
        Great Spirit.

Smokin'

Say, he don' smokin', jus' to smokin',
    Ol' Injun, long 'go,
Like he's do eva' body, eva'wha' now days.
    Jus' puff, puffin' so.

Long 'go, Injun', he's thinkin an thinkin'
    'Bout word he's want to sent,
To Great Spirit, somethin' it's good one
    To help 'im, what it's meant;
        Then he's smokin' plenty.

He don' sed nothin', jus' smokin' an think
    Jus' 'bout that what he's want.
He's do this way long time, himse'f,
    'Til he's sure it's that way.

Don' tole nobody 'bout it but jus' hese'f,
    'Cause too much talk no good.
Whiteman he's smart, but not foun' that out yet,
    'Spec' so no b'lieve it, if he could.

"Put it in you pipe an smoke it,"
    I hear 'im, whiteman say.
It's jus' how he's do, Ol' Injun,
    Meb' so, 'at's how he pray.

'Cause he don' like it to talk to Great Spirit,
    An tole 'Im it, what mus' do,
So he's think it, an smoke carry thinkin'
        Eva'wha', up wha' looks blue.

BIG TREE'S HOUSE

Ol' Big Tree, he's bin down this way,
He's tole me 'bout it, his horse.
It's kin' a "baw-ky", how you say?
Jus' stan'in', won't go, of course.

He say it's all a time makes 'im mad,
That horse, 'cause it's don' want go;
Sometime he's want a work prit' bad,
An that horse he's stan' jus' so.

Otha' day, he's plow in squaw-corn patch,
'Long side big road, down tha'.
That horse jus' stan', don' move one scratch;
Big Tree, he's cuss 'im but horse don' ca'.

By-um-by it's comin' down a road,
That place, Big Tree, he's plow,
Big noise, it's what you call 'im, Foad,
Lots a rattle, it's ol one, now.

It's come right wha' he's stan', that horse.
He's jump, Big Tree heap holla' whoa;
That horse he's plenty scare of course,
Don' lis'n to Big Tree, jus' keep on go.

Big Tree he's go prit' hurry up too,
'Cause it's lines tie togetha, 'roun' back.
He's pull on lines, but that don' do,
He's jus' got to folla' in track.

He's tell it, Big Tree, an he's say:
"Horse heap dam' fool', that's the one;
Sometime he's go, sometime he's stay,
He's jus' too 'nuff or too none."

A Borrowed Tale

Say, you know that time that Ol' Otta'
He's slide down that mount'in from th' sky?
Well, he's wored it jus' all a fur off his tail,
Jus' smoof, an skin looks ugly an a' dry.

He's sure feel sorrow, 'cause it's always bin,
He's kin' o' proud o' that tail jus' all a time,
'Cause it's always bin cova' jus' nice sof' fur,
An it's looks good draggin' long bellin'.

Don' got none, nobody, 'at looks so fine,
'Less it's Mus'rat, his jus' 'bout nex' best;
He's sure feelin' prit' bad, 'at Ol' Otta',
'Cause now his tail it's look bad, 'mongst th' rest.

He's jus' stay at home, don' went no-wha'
'Cause he's shame how it's spoil it, 'at tail;
It's look so bad, he's think eva'body laughin',
If they seen 'im comin' down a trail.

But it's "Rah-shu" come 'long an tole 'im,
'Bout big council, down a lake, he's haf to go;
He don' sed it nothin', jus' like thinkin',
Then he's start it, like he's know what's goin' to do.

Mus'rat, he's not b'long to that big council,
So Ol' Otta' he's go to Mus'rat, his lodge.
That fella he's sittin' outside singin'
But when he's see Ol' Otta', he's dodge, In a wata'.

Ol' Otta' couldn' seen 'im nowha', Mus'rat,
So he's holla': "Ho' my fren', I like spoke to you now;
I like to borrow'd you' tail, to wear big council;
We could swap 'til I come back, I tole you how,

Mus'rat, he's good fella, so he's sed it, "A'right!"
An he's swap with him his tail, that Ol' Otta'
By-um-by he's look behin' 'im, see that tail
      An he's so scare,
He's jus' hurry tumble ova' in a wata'
        To hide it that tail.

Ol' Otta' he's go down a road, kin' a chuckle, feelin' good;
It's look good, that Mus'rat tail, draggin' tha' behin'.
So he's go to that big council, jus' feelin' kin' o' proud;
But he neva' did gif back to him, his tail, that Mus'rat,
   An he's eva' since stay in a wata'
     Mus'rat.

The Warrior's Plume[4]

On the plains and in the vales of Oklahoma,
    Grew a flower of the Tyrian hue,
The color that is loved by the Redman,
    That tells him light and life,
        And love are true.

Long ago it flamed in beauty on the prairies,
    Lighting reaching vistas with its glow;
Ere advent of the whiteman and his fences,
    Told the care-free, roving hunter
        He must go.
The throng, the herd, and greed have madly trampled

Prairie, woodland, valley, and the height;
Crushed the feath'ry flower and rudely blighted
    Its pride and life and beauty,
        And its light.

Today 'tis found in silent glades and meadows
    Where by twos and threes it greets the May.
Like the scattered braves who loved its color,
    It has passed, been trodden out
        Along the way.

As the oriflamme it flaunted through past ages
    Went to gladden the fairness of the earth;
So the greatness of the Indian will linger
    In the land that loves them both
        And gave them birth.

---

4. The Scarlet Painted Cup was called by the Wyandots, the Warrior's Plume.

A Mojave Lullaby

Sleep, my little man-child,
Dream-time to you has come.

In the closely matted branches
Of the mesquite tree,
The mother-bird has nestled
Her little ones; see
From the ghost-hills of your fathers,
Purpling shadows eastward crawl,
While beyond the western sky-tints pale,
As twilight spreads its pall.

The eastern hills are lighted,
See their sharp peaks burn and glow,
With the colors the Great Sky-Chief
Gave your father for his bow.

Hush my man-child; be not frighted,
'Tis the father's step draws nigh
O'er the trail along the river,
Where the arrow-weeds reach high
Above his dark head, see
He parts them with his strong hands,
As he steps forth into view.
He is coming home to mother,
Home to mother and to you.

Sleep my little man-child,
Daylight has gone.
There's no twitter in the branches,
Dream-time has come.

Coyote

Yo-ho, Little Medicine Brother in gray,
    Yo-ho, I am list'ning to your call
As it comes from the edge of th' chapparral,
    And I wonder, what is that you say.

Now your voice is fain't, it sounds far away.
    Are you telling of the coming of friends?
Or do you say that the bison-herd wends
    Hitherward, is distant but a day?
Now your notes are broken, sharp, and clear,
    Warning of the coming of the foe;
Of their warriors and their spears I must know,
    And must reckon by your yelps if they're near.

When your tones quaver low like a child,
    I know that gaunt famine cometh nigh;
And you shiver on your hummock closely by,
    As you scent the grim, gray norther wild.

A DESERT MEMORY

Lonely, open, vast and free,
The dark'ning desert lies;
The wind sweeps o'er it fiercely,
And the yellow sand flies.
The tortuous trail is hidden,
Ere the sand-storm has passed
With all its wild, mad shriekings,
Borne shrilly on its blast.

Are they fiends or are they demons
That wail weirdly as they go,
Those hoarse and dismal cadences,
From out their depths of woe?
Will they linger and enfold
The lone trav'ler in their spell,

Weave 'roun'd him incantations,
Brewed and bro't forth from their hell?
Bewilder him and turn him
From the rugged, hidden trail,
Make him wander far and falter,
And tremblingly quail
At the desert and the loneliness
So fearful and so grim,
That to his fervid fancy,
Wraps in darkness only him?

The wind has spent its fierce wild wail,
    The dark storm-pall has shifted,
Forth on his sight the 'stars gleam pale
    In the purpling haze uplifted.

And down the steep trail, as he lists,
    He hears soft music stealing;
It trembling falls through filmy mists,
    From rock-walls fain't echoes pealing.

Whence comes this mystic night-song
With its rhythm wild and free,
With its pleading and entreaty
Pouring forth upon the 'sea
Of darkness, vast and silent,
Like a tiny ray of hope
That oft-times comes to comfort
When in sorrow's depths we grope?

'Tis the An-gu, the Kat-ci-na,
'Tis the Hopi's song of prayer,
That in darkness wards off danger,
When 'tis breathed in the air;
Over desert, butte, and mesa,
It is borne out on the night,
Dispelling fear and danger,
Driving evil swift a-flight.

An Indian Love Song

Light o' the lodge, how I love thee,
Light o' the lodge, how I love thee,
    Mianza, my wild-wood fawn!
To wait and to watch for thy passing.
    On hill-top I linger at dawn.

Glimmer of morn, how I love thee,
Glimmer of morn, how I love thee!
    My flute to the ground now I fling,
    As you tread the 'steep trail to the spring,
For thy coming has silenced my song.

Shimmer of moon on the river,
Sheen of soft star on the lake!
    Moonlight and starlight are naught;
    Their gleam and their glow is ne'er fraught
With such love-light as falls from thine eyes.

A Wyandot Cradle Song

Hush thee and sleep, little one,
    The feathers on thy board sway to and fro;
The shadows reach far downward in the water
    The great old owl is waking, day will go.

Rest thee and fear not, little one,
    Flitting fireflies come to light you on your way
To the fair land of dreams, while in the grasses
    The happy cricket chirps his merry lay.
Tsa-du-meh[5] watches always o'er her little one.
    The great owl cannot harm you, slumber on
'Till the pale light comes shooting from the eastward,
    And the twitter of the birds says night has gone.

---

5. Hi-a-stah, Wyandot for Father. Tsa-du-meh, Wyandot for Mother.

Wyandot Names

"O-he-zhuh!" 'At's how sed it, Wyandots;
"O-hee-oh!" 'At's how say, Frenchman;
"O-hi-o!" 'At's how sed it, Long Knives;
      'An it's mean, beautiful riva'.

"To-roon-toh!" 'At's what 'say, ol' Wyandots;
"To-ron-toh!" 'At's what call it, French;
"To-ron-to!" 'At's what 'say, British;
      'An it's mean, great rock standing.

"Sci-non-to!" It's that way in Wyandot;
"Sci-yun-toh!" 'At's what 'sed, French;
"Sci-o-to!" 'At's how sed Long Knives;
      'An it's mean, plenty deer.

Huntin'

Win' it's in a south,
Kin' a cloudy in a sky.
Good time to huntin'
Spec' I go by-um-by.

Looks kin' a smoky
All 'roun' a edge,
Spec' could fin' it, rabbit,
Down tha' 'long a hedge.

'Way down a Sycamo',
Wha' that ridge look blue,
You could fin' it buck o' doe,
Oh, fifty years 'go.

An 'way cross that valley,
Wha' that timba thicken,
Early in a mornin'
Lots a pra'rie chicken.

Ova' that long ridge,
Wha' sky seem kin' a murky,
You could hear 'em callin'
Plenty big wil' turkey.

Duck, down on Gran' Riva'
Flyin' looks like cloud,
Sometime you could heard 'im,
He's quack plenty loud.

Sometime come wil pige'un,
He's fly two-three day,
Must a be fo' milli'un
'Fo he's all gon 'way.

HEN-TOH

Oh, lots a games them days.
You could prit' nea' grab it.
Now, can jus' go down a road
An mebbe so fin' rabbit.

Triplets

It's in Ohio, Shawnee town, all same time they born:
  Te-cum-tha, La-lee-wah-see-ka, an littl' 'notha one.
He's die that 'notha one, jus' when he's born,
  That las' one, poo'h littl' boy.
That fatha' that motha', both Sha-wah-no-ro-noh,
  They b'long that band what come from fa' south,
Come back to ol huntin' grounds an they own peoples,
  Cause Injun always like do that way;
  But got none huntin' grounds, now.

Great mans them two, Te-cum-tha, La-lee-wah-see-ka,
  Great chief, warriors, leader of all they peoples.
That las' one, he's Shawnee Prophet,
  An he's see what's goin' do whitemans.
Te-cum-tha[6] he's great warrior; La-lee-wah-see-ka,
  He's big leader, always think of many things;
But shucks! It's too many whitemans.
  Two mouse can't eat it big cornfield,
    An it's too many whitemans, yet.

Mebbe so he's live otha' one, poo'h littl' fella,
  Three of it could done mo' betta' 'an jus' two;
But leva', min', I guess no use, cause whitemans,
  He's jus' want what Injuns got yet;
    An he ain' got it much, eitha'.

---

6. Te-cum-tha (ordinary English form Tecumseh) and the Shawnee Prophet, were two of triplets, the third dying at birth.

Sleep It Summa' Time

Eva' sleep it out a' doors, you,
    Just on the ground? It's you motha'.
Could look up at sky, it's kin' a blue,
        Little sta's look at each otha,
           And wink 'em little bit,
                Ain't it?

Wonda' what made it, all them sta'?
        'Spec' it's little bits of sun broke it off;
'Cause he's run fas', and he's go fa',
        And 'spec' sometimes the road's mighty rough.
           Might be that kin',
                Ain't it?

Sometimes little breeze, he's blow cool'.
        Feel good, make it f-i-n-e sleep it
I like that kin', I don't fool';
        Fella got sof' bed could keep it.
           Don't want that kin', me,
                Ain't it?

Them fella's bug what a singin'
        Up in a tree, go siz-z-z,
Soun's like a nice, that ringin';
        Make it good sleep; gee whizz!
           I could sleep it 'summa' time,
                Ain't it?

August

'Bout come daylight, it's sky kin' a blue,
An all 'roun' edges, mo' blue an smokey;
It's kin' a chilly col', and it's shiva', you
When you jus' move 'roun' kin' a pokey.

Hills 'way off, it's look kin' a nice,
An you jus' like to stan' an look
Once fa' as you could, an mebbe so, twice,
Seems jus' like picture in a book.

Only picture, it couldn' make it that good,
'Cause Great Spirit, He's make it that one;
You could see wha's riva', valley, an a wood,
Ova', tha' wha' he's comin' up, son.

By-um-by, when sun, he's get up straight,
It's a h-o-t, you don' shiva', jus' want a laid
On a nice sof' grasses down tha' by th' gate,
Unda' big black-jack trees, in a shade, 'Ain't it?

"WEENGK"[7]

"Weengk, he's lit'l fella make you sleep it,
You can't seen 'im, you eye too big.
He's hidin' eva' wha' an he's keep it
Dance all a time, what you call it,—jig.

He's carry lit'l war-club, hit 'em on head,
Eva'body, anywha', make 'em sleepy come,
You can't stayed wake 'em, go jus' like dead,
An Weengk fin' 'notha' fella, hit him some.

He's you fren', that Weengk, 'at's a fac',
Eva'body got to sleep it, now an then;
But mebbe so, he's jump it on you back,
When you hunt it, an jus' got to shoot 'gen.

It's bad lucks that one, deer run 'way,
Cause can't shoot it good if make feel lazy,
But that fella, he's come, jus' anytime a day,
An you sure want sleep it like you crazy."

---

7. "Weengk" is the Odjibwa Spirit of Sleep.

A Song of a Navajo Weaver

For ages long, my people have been
    Dwellers in this land;
For ages viewed these mountains,
    Loved these mesas and these sands,
That stretch afar and glisten,
    Glimmering in the sun
As it lights the mighty canons
    Ere the weary day is done.
Shall I, a patient dweller in this
    Land of fair blue skies,
Tell something of their story while
    My shuttle swiftly flies?
As I weave I'll trace their journey,
    Devious, rough and wandering,
Ere they reached the silent region
    Where the night stars seem to sing.
When the myriads of them glitter
    Over peak and desert waste,
Crossing which the silent runner and
    The gaunt co-yo-tees haste.
Shall I weave the zig-zag pathway
    Whence the sacred lire was born;
And interweave the symbol of the God
    Who brought the corn—
Of the Rain-God whose fierce anger
    Was appeased by sacred meal,
And the trust that my brave people
    In him evermore shall feel?
All this perhaps I might weave
    As the woof goes to and fro,
Wafting as my shuttle passes,
    Humble hopes, and joys and care,
Weaving closely, weaving slowly,
    While I watch the pattern grow;
Showing somethin'g of my life:
    To the Spirit God a prayer.

Grateful that he brought my people
     To the land of silence vast;
Taught them arts of peace and ended
     All their wanderings of the past.
Deftly now I trace the figures,
     This of joy and that of woe;
And I leave an open gateway
     For the Dau[8] to come and go.

---

8. There is an irregularity in every design woven into a Navajo blanket, thus leaving a place for the "Dau" or spirit of the blanket to go out and in.

ARROW-HEADS

Bit by bit with tireless effort.
    Was the hard flint flaked to form
        Tip for shaft and spear-head
            Long ago.

Time was counted naught in those days,
    And the end sufficed the needs
        Of the patient worker
            For his bow.

Skilled in craft of plain and mountain,
    He must ever be alert,
        In the haunts of bison,
            Or of deer.

On the shores of lake and river,
    Trod his moccasin'd foot,
        As he sought shy quarry
            For his spear.

Lithe of limb with might of muscle,
    Swiftly wends he o'er the portage,
        Shoulders bearing lightly
            His canoe.

Should he meet a wily foeman,
    As he treads the darksome glades
        His the need to dare then
            And to do.

Thoughts like these come as we wander
    O'er the fallowed fields and find
        In our path an old
            Arrow-head.

And we form in fervid fancy,
　　As we scan th' enduring flint,
　　　A measure of those brave
　　　　Warriors dead.

BIG KNIFE

Joe Bigknife he's liv'd ova' on a Spring Riva'
He's had ferry at th' Ol' Jim Charley Ford.
Joe, he's tallest one of them Injun Police,
An if he's sed it somethin' he's mean it eva' word,
 Tho' he don' talk it all a time, eitha'.

His house it's jus' 'bout half a mile 'way
From ferry an the ford, it's by th' hill.
If riva's up, he's at th' house, could seen it comin' team;
Comin' otha' way, they holla', an jus' wait until
 Joe, he's come took 'em ova' on th' ferry.

It's summa' time, evenin', it's a fella comin' south,
He's comin down to riva', stop, an give a shout.
Joe, he's answa' from th' house, but he's kin' a slow,
Man, he's got big hurry, try th' ford, an jus' pull out,
 When Joe, he's comin' down to th' riva'.

Joe sed it: "Whiteman, you too hurry. Don' I sed it
I come all a time if you holla'? I mean it what I say."
An he's pull it out his gun, then sed it 'notha' 'gen:
"Now turn it 'roun' you wagon, you go back 'gen otha' way,
 It's kin' a deep, but 'spec' you make it, anyhow.

"I come ova' in a boat, prit' soon, an brought you back."
'At's what he's done it, Joe, an fella sed: "How much?"
Joe sed it: "Keep it you' money, white man; nex' time
Don' hollered, you don' want a me come, cause such
 Kin' a way, I don't like it that kin.'

"Dam' fool', sometimes drowned you wagon, eva'thing,
Tryin' cross a riva', when it's wata' it's too deep.
Now betta' pull it out, you got so hurry.
Betta' drive it on quick, cause mebbe I can't keep
 From sayin' somethin' 'fo' you go."

HEN-TOH

Agency Police II

High Waters

Bearskin, he's live down on Grand Riva',
Gilstrap Ferry, on ol' Military Road,
Goin' south, down to Ol' Fort Gibson.
It's been lots a rainin', 'bout one week.
Bearskin, he's in Seneca, he's tradin',
Talkin' 'bout a weather with Murdock,
Bearskin, he's sed it:
    "Oh, rain just' like a hell;
Fall down jus' like pour out a bucket.
Riva' it's a high like a tree."

AGENCY POLICE III

WINNEY

It's Winney, he's one a them Injun Pol'eez,
Sometimes he's got kin' a braggin' way.
It's a bunch a fellas stanin' out by a trees,
An Winney he's tole 'em one day:
"I neva' did cock it whiteman on my pistol, yet."[9]
       Notha''Gen.

It's issue day at Agency, an all them fellas on hand,
Winney, jus' kin' a braggin', he's talkn' 'bout Splitlog Band:
"Y' oughta' heard it, maybe pooty moosics,
Me, I play it 'secon' alto, jus' easy to blow.

Whitetree, he's got it, that b-i-g drum,
He's hit 'im, 'bout bust 'im, it's go bum, bum, bum.
We got it lit'l book, lots a tune, Nellie Gray,
An Red an White an Blue,
An tha' Gran'fatha Clocks, he's a dandy.
Bes' one of all of it tho', le's see, it's numba' eight,
It's a p-o-o-t-y one, you bet'cha:
Yankey Dool'ey; sweet as fo' honey, ain't it, Whitetree?

---

9. He intended to say, "I never did cock my pistol on a white man yet." To understand,
insert pause after "on."

HEN-TOH

A Note About the Author

Bertrand N.O. Walker, better known by his Wyandot name Hen-Toh (1870–1927) was a Native American author and poet. Born in Kansas City, Kansas, Walker was a member of the Oklahoma band of the Big Turtle Clan and received his education from a Friends' Mission School. Walker spent the entirety of his life working in the Indian Service, spending his early years as a teacher and clerk and his later years focused on his writing and family. Though his literary output was limited to a volume of poetry, *Yon-Doo-Shah-We-Ah (Nubbins),* and book of Native folklore, *Tales of the Bark Lodges* (1924), Walker's contributions to the preservation of Wyandot culture have been appreciated by generations of researchers and readers alike.

A Note from the Publisher

Spanning many genres, from non-fiction essays to literature classics to children's books and lyric poetry, Mint Edition books showcase the master works of our time in a modern new package. The text is freshly typeset, is clean and easy to read, and features a new note about the author in each volume. Many books also include exclusive new introductory material. Every book boasts a striking new cover, which makes it as appropriate for collecting as it is for gift giving. Mint Edition books are only printed when a reader orders them, so natural resources are not wasted. We're proud that our books are never manufactured in excess and exist only in the exact quantity they need to be read and enjoyed.

bookfinity & MINT EDITIONS

Enjoy more of your favorite classics with Bookfinity,
a new search and discovery experience for readers.
With Bookfinity, you can discover more vintage
literature for your collection, find your Reader Type,
track books you've read or want to read,
and add reviews to your favorite books.
Visit www.bookfinity.com, and click on
Take the Quiz to get started.

Don't forget to follow us
@bookfinityofficial and @mint_editions

bookfinity™

Discover more of your favorite classics with Bookfinity™.

- Track your reading with custom book lists.
- Get great book recommendations for your personalized Reader Type.
- Add reviews for your favorite books.
- AND MUCH MORE!

Visit **bookfinity.com** and take the fun Reader Type quiz to get started.

Enjoy our classic and modern companion pairings!

Printed in the USA
CPSIA information can be obtained
at www.ICGtesting.com
JSHW021303231023
50684JS00004B/62